SPYMASTERS

CLIFFORD RILEY

SCHOLASTIC INC.

Clifford Riley wishes to acknowledge
the following Cahills:

Gavin Brown

Christina McTighe

Jackie Reitzes

The 39 Clues: Cahill Files #2: The Submarine Job (978-0-545-45729-3)
© 2012 Scholastic Inc.
The 39 Clues: Cahill Files #3: The Redcoat Chase (978-0-545-45730-9)
© 2012 Scholastic Inc.
The 39 Clues: Cahill Files #4: The Houdini Escape (978-0-545-45731-6)
© 2012 Scholastic Inc.

This collection first printing, May 2013

ISBN 978-0-545-56468-7

10 9 8 7 6 5 4 3   13 14 15 16 17 18

Cover: vault and background © jamesbenet/istockphoto; gold disk © J. Helgason/Shutterstock; small bolts © Spectral Design/Shutterstock; texture for text panel © optimarc/Shutterstock; Endpapers: texture for text panel © optimarc/Shutterstock; small bolts – Spectral Design/Shutterstock; magnets – Scholastic Art; Houdini – Library of Congress; nautilus – U.S. Navy, Submarine Force Museum

Printed in the U.S.A.   23

Scholastic US: 557 Broadway • New York, NY 10012
Scholastic Canada: 604 King Street West • Toronto, ON M5V 1E1
Scholastic New Zealand Limited: Private Bag 94407 • Greenmount, Manukau 2141
Scholastic UK Ltd.: Euston House • 24 Eversholt Street • London NW1 1DB

To whom it may concern,

The information in this book comes from the Cahill vault, which means that *none* of it was meant for your eyes. Over the past 500 years, a number of exceedingly dangerous items have been placed in the vault for safekeeping—assassination orders, confession-filled diaries, treasure maps, and many other items that I know better than to list here. Documents that have sparked wars, incited revolutions, and led to the downfall of governments, kings, and empires.

It was *not* my idea to make this material public. I was given specific instructions by my former employer, William McIntyre, to protect the information in the vault. However, after recent, tragic events, it looks like I'm taking orders from someone new—someone who believes that the Cahill Files are essential to the security of the Cahill family . . . and the world at large.

And so, the vault has been opened. Do with these stories what you will. But when you find yourself weighed down by the secrets and scandals that shaped history, just remember one thing: I told you so.

Clifford Riley

THE REDCOAT CHASE

PART 1

Maryland, 1814

Frederick Warren knew he shouldn't do it. He knew his parents would be angry, and that he would be punished and told he was too old for childish pranks. But he could worry about punishment after the fact. At that moment, on a dark August dawn, Frederick needed a good hard laugh to lighten the mood. And what his parents didn't know wouldn't hurt them.

It was 1814, and America had been at war for two years with no sign of the conflict letting up. Everyone was feeling the effects — soaring prices of food, a constant shortage of money, and living with the threat that, at any time, the British could attack.

Frederick's parents had seemed particularly frayed lately, his mother taking care of guests at their Maryland inn with resignation, sighing as she spooned stews at night or stirred porridge in the morning. All Frederick's father could talk about was the course of the war, which pressed closer and closer to their doorsteps, the British army advancing more each day. It seemed to Frederick that no one had smiled in years, let alone laughed.

So earlier that morning, before his mother readied breakfast, Frederick carefully replaced the sugar in his mother's fancy pewter sugar bowls with salt. Now, as he brewed a pot of tea and stacked a tower of golden toast on a tray for their crabbiest guest, Frederick chuckled to himself. His parents had been preoccupied that morning and hadn't noticed his little trick. Their town hall meetings had been starting earlier and earlier before the sun rose, and pressing later and later into the night, too. The inn responsibilities were increasingly falling to Frederick.

This week alone, his parents had been laboring over sketches for evacuation maps and serving on committees planning what to do should the British reach town—where to take shelter, where to find stashed food, the least conspicuous back roads out of town. Frederick wasn't sure where his parents received their information, or why they were always the first to find out everything. It seemed to Frederick that his parents were always whom other people turned to when they needed to be comforted, when they needed a plan in times of crisis, and, most of all, when they needed information no one else could seem to get.

In the breakfast room, Frederick deposited the tray in front of a scowling old woman and her husband, who were traveling through town to get to Washington.

After Frederick had served the woman the night before, he'd heard her mutter to her husband, "If our army is as sloppy as the staff at this inn, we'll all be singing 'God Save the King' before the year is out."

Now Frederick bowed lavishly and left for the kitchen, where he peeked out from behind the doorway to watch. The old woman nibbled on some toast and loudly declared it burnt to her husband, who shrugged and ate it anyway. The woman then spooned three helpings of what she thought was sugar into her bowl of tea. She blew on the steam that rose up from the bowl and inhaled the scent before bringing the tea to her lips and taking a long warm sip. Not a split second later, the woman's tea came flying at her husband as a liquid projectile right into his face. He leapt to his feet and wiped his face with a handkerchief.

"Constance, you forget yourself!" he huffed at his wife, her face puckered and furious.

The other guests, seated at nearby tables, were trying visibly not to laugh.

Frederick, who'd seen the whole thing from his perch just inside the doorway of the kitchen, doubled over, holding his stomach, tears leaking from his eyes.

The old woman gesticulated wildly, knocking the bowl of sugar onto the floor. "It's salt! SALT!" she screeched, though it was clear her husband had no idea what she was talking about. "WHO DID THIS?"

Frederick took a cautious step toward the kitchen just as his mother came in from outside, untying her bonnet and setting down a pail of fresh cream. Her eyes were pinched and exhausted, and she looked at Frederick wearily, as if to say, *I don't have the energy for this right now.*

Frederick dared one last peek into the dining room and caught the expression on the face of the woman's husband, who was trying very hard to suppress a smile.

The barn smelled of manure. Frederick had to shovel it, sweep the barn floor, and then milk, feed, and water the cow until she relieved herself and it was time to shovel again. *Whose bright idea was it, again*, Frederick chided himself, *to switch the salt and the sugar?* His parents had berated him, but what made him feel worse was that they'd been forced to return the old woman's money, which Frederick hadn't even considered until it was too late. His prank had been poor judgment, Frederick agreed, and no amount of shoveling would replace the funds his parents had lost.

It was already bright and hot, even though it was not yet noon. Frederick wiped his brow with his handkerchief.

As he worked, Frederick's thoughts turned again to the war. Even decades after the War of Independence, England was *still* trying to turn America back into a British colony. They had blockaded American ports for their own selfish gains in the war against Napoleon.

And then they'd impressed American sailors, kidnapping them at sea and enlisting them to fight on British ships!

Frederick hadn't been alive during the War of Independence, but when he was younger he would press his ear to the floor to try and overhear the war stories his father told of the battlefield — men getting blown up, shot down, sliced in two with a bayonet, how they taught those redcoats a lesson and won freedom for all the land. As far as Frederick was concerned, the British were the most villainous people alive.

The barn shared a wall with the small stable, and Frederick could hear the thud of horses kicking in their stalls. He'd need to feed and water them later.

Frederick drove his shoulder into his work, lifting a pitchfork heavy with hay into his wheelbarrow. The haystacks loomed tall, and there were a lot of horses to feed. Sunlight streamed in through the doorway; it was already midmorning. What if he wasn't finished by supper? He decided maybe he'd like to lie down on the haystack, just to rest his back for one moment. He could have sworn his eyes hadn't been closed a second when —

"Frederick! Wake up, son!"

Frederick shook his bleary head awake, confused at the sight of his father looming above him. He flushed in embarrassment. In his exile in the barn, Frederick had hoped to gain back his parents' trust, not further erode it.

"F-Father," Frederick stammered, "I didn't mean to fall asleep. I'll make sure the chores—"

But his father wasn't paying attention to the barn. He had a look on his face that Frederick had never seen before, and was pushing his hair back and forth while holding his hat in his other hand.

"I apologize, again, for this morning—" Frederick began, but his father cut him off, which was also a first. Frederick's father believed in a man's sense of dignity. He considered it a breach of manners to interrupt someone.

"There isn't time, son," his father said, his voice barely audible, sounding higher and less certain than Frederick had ever heard it, like a child afraid of the dark. His father was wearing his black waistcoat and jacket with black leggings—the outfit he normally reserved for funerals. A chill ran through Frederick. His father's rifle, which was normally stored away, was propped against the barn door.

"What is it, Father?" Frederick asked. He brushed off his pants and straightened up, rising from the haystacks to try and meet his father's eyes.

"Son, what I am about to tell you may not make sense right now, but you must listen. You must be serious, for once."

Frederick braced himself; everything that was sturdy this morning now felt uncertain, shaky. *Serious, for once:* The words clattered around in his head. Did his father really think him so frivolous?

"Your mother and I—we are not innkeepers." He paused here, and met Frederick's eyes. "Well, we are, of course, but that is not our main work. We have a special heritage—*you* have a special heritage. You are a member of the Cahills, a family that goes back hundreds of years. We're Madrigals, members of a group of elite Cahills."

"But I'm a Warren!" Frederick protested.

His father toed at the ground with his boot, and the nervous tic in someone normally so composed made Frederick uneasy.

"Yes, but you're also part of a powerful secret organization. We don't just run our inn for travelers. It's also a place of safety for other Cahills, a place they can escape their enemies."

"Enemies?" Frederick asked. A chill ran up his spine.

His father nodded. "The Vespers. Those who seek to extinguish us, forever."

Frederick gasped a sharp breath—*extinguish us*?

His father put an unsteady hand on Frederick's shoulder, and his brow furrowed as he forced himself to continue. He swallowed mightily. "At this very moment, son, there is an extremely dangerous man in the area. A Vesper traveling with the British army here in Maryland. Your mother and I must find him and stop him, or—" Frederick's father broke off and gave his son an anguished look.

Frederick's head was spinning now. Everything was tilting—the way he felt dizzy after circling the maypole too many times the past spring, when the ground came up and knocked the wind out of him.

"Where are you going?" Frederick managed to ask.

"It doesn't matter. What does matter is keeping you out of harm's way."

Frederick took stock of his father's face — the silvery hair, watery blue eyes, the quiet lines around his eyes and smile, a gentleman's face, a distinguished retired soldier, to be sure, but this man, *this* man, was also a — would that make him a spy? It was inconceivable. He tried to memorize all of the details of his father's face, searching it, as if it were the first time he was really seeing it. *Please, please, let it not be the last.*

Soft footsteps on the grass broke their reverie. Frederick's mother hurried across the barnyard to join them, chickens squawking at her as she passed — a harsh, grating sound. She wore her good walking dress and gloves, with her straw bonnet tied under her chin. She clutched her shawl around herself tightly, as if to protect herself from a blizzard, even though it was the height of summer.

Frederick's mother took his arm in her own and asked if he understood the grave danger that they were all in.

"No," Frederick answered helplessly. "And you can't tell me what's going on?"

His mother's lip quivered as she shook her head and turned to look at his father.

"Is there nothing I can do?" Frederick asked

desperately. "Have I disappointed you somehow, this morning—?"

"Son," she whispered, turning to face him, "if we felt it would be safer for you to join us, we would bring you. Your safety is our greatest priority. We're doing this to *protect* you, and not only you, but to safeguard our innocent neighbors against these terrible people. Can you see that?"

Frederick shrugged.

"Listen to me," she said, her voice hitting an urgent note, her arms on his shoulders, her hands squeezing for emphasis. "If you hear *any*thing about the British approaching, take to the church *immediately*, and hide, do you hear me? Follow their guidelines for taking shelter until you can safely evacuate. I need you to promise me you'll do this, son. I won't leave without knowing you're safe."

"But the British won't, they're not going to—"

And then his mother started to cry, hot swift tears that made Frederick's chest ache. She said, "You have to promise me. Promise me?"

"Yes," he said as she embraced him, finality in her grip, "I promise I will run at the first sign of the British approaching."

He wasn't sure when he'd grown to be taller than her, but his mother felt frail in his arms, and he could barely keep himself from crushing her with the strength of his good-bye.

Father could never withstand emotional scenes;

they upset him too greatly ever since his brother died from a British bullet. With a handshake that squeezed too hard, Father commanded Frederick to keep himself safe before quitting the barn for the stables, where he rattled a stall door open. They could hear him mounting Buster in a swift motion of boots in stirrups, and then the clomp of horseshoes on the gravel as he rode to the edge of the drive. Buster stamped impatiently as they waited for Frederick's mother.

She took a final look at Frederick before swinging up behind his father. Frederick watched as they galloped away together, out of sight.

Entirely alone, Frederick's face heated up and his heart started kicking, the barn seeming to swim before him. What was it his father had called them—*Cahills?* And the enemies—*Vespers?* The war was blazing nearby, so close that just the day before he'd seen an amputee carried out of the town doctor's house. So close that he'd read about a Chesapeake town being raided and looted by the British. What if the Vespers came for him, now, all alone, and he didn't have time to escape? And on top of it all, that stupid prank—what if that was the last memory his parents ever had of him? *You must be serious, for once.*

Frederick threw the pitchfork across the barn, and watched it sail through the air before crashing to the floor.

The British were coming!

"And, in conclusion, madam,"

of messengers, both coated in dust

den straight from the battle near Blade

come to bid you flee, per your husband'

are not safe here, as the British are eage

ate us and the President's House is their prir

They'll be here in a few short hours! They seek

the Capitol, too, and God knows what else. We're

to escort you to safety."

Dolley Madison, the first lady of the United State

looked up from the Cabinet papers she was clutch-

ing only to push away a strand of hair that had come

loose from her otherwise immaculate bun. Then she

returned to the boxes strewn around her on the floor.

"Gentlemen," she said, skimming over the docu-

ments before her, "that won't be necessary."

She looked up only long enough to see the two mes-

sengers' mouths drop at the same time, as if they were

puppets controlled by some higher hand.

The air in the library was hot. The room, which was

also her husband's office, was paneled in mahogany.

Grand floor-to-ceiling bookshelves ran the length of the

room, with stepladders on wheels mounted to them to

more easily get from book to book. The books took up

all of the shelves, some stacked sideways, but, far from

looking cluttered or disorganized, the disarray gave the

impression of being at a crowded and happy party.

There were green velvet chaise lounges with gold

verlooking the President's

the room, on top of a

es's desk, flanked by

re the boxes and

ne of them con-

d to find. *This*

dth time. As

station it had

ny young lives it had

member of an elite branch

ne knew that the repercussions of

would be far worse than anyone imag-

esper had insinuated himself into the highest

nks of the British army, and if he were allowed to

succeed . . . Dolley put the nasty thought firmly out of her mind.

She was losing time with every second the messengers continued to bother her, and she needed to focus on the task at hand. A Madrigal contact had told her that there was a map somewhere in the President's House, a map leading to a small gold ring that the Vespers coveted above all things. The Madrigals had never been sure what the importance of the ring was, but they had sworn to keep it out of Vesper hands. As soon as Dolley learned that the British were in the area, she'd sent an urgent message to her contact, alerting him that the map was in danger. But help from the Madrigals had never arrived, and Dolley

said one of a pair

having just rid-

nsburg, "we've

request. You

to humili-

ne target.

to burn

here

had to face the fact that her message hadn't gotten through. It was up to her to keep the map out of Vesper hands—if only she could discover where it was.

Her fingers paged rapidly through the papers in front of her as sweat beaded her forehead and coated her throat.

"Madam," said the older messenger, "leave these papers be. You need to collect your own belongings so I can escort you to your husband. We don't have much time! Are you not afraid?" The younger of the two messengers shuffled his feet.

Dolley didn't look up from her task. "Very much so. I'm afraid for the sake of the army, and the sake of the country. My personal safety is far less important when our nation is in crisis."

There was a trunk set up next to the desk, in which Dolley had placed documents tied with string—pamphlets from before the revolution, the correspondence of past presidents. She'd packed them in to maximize space in the deep heavy trunk, the eighth she'd filled that day. Dolley had already searched two rooms methodically, packing up national treasures to whisk away to safety when she finally found the map and could flee. She was already running low on trunks. And wagons for carting them to safety. And people to drive the wagons and guard the President's House.

"Madam!" the older messenger cried again, watching her hustle back and forth through the room, her skirt trailing on the floor and picking up dust from all the books and old paper. She rolled a document between two scrolls and placed it in the trunk.

"Madam!" he repeated. "You have received a direct order from the commander in chief. It is *he* who said you must evacuate. The Cabinet papers are not as valuable as your life!" He slammed his palm on the grand mahogany table.

Dolley stopped in her tracks. Her life? Her thoughts darted to her dear sister, whom she'd written earlier that morning. The image of her son John's face appeared before her now, all handsome and grown. She wanted to see him start a family one day. A wave of despair washed over her, and for a moment she was ready to drop everything and run out with these men, to leave everything behind.

But then her eyes scanned the gorgeous room and settled on the American flag in the corner, its stars and stripes bright and bold. Even in the depth of this humid heat wave, they sent goose bumps down her skin. The fate of the nation was at stake, everything they'd built so carefully. The British were bad enough, but the Vespers were the enemy of free men everywhere. Dolley searched inside herself for courage. If she left, she would be allowing something unspeakable to win. And all her life she would watch on, knowing that she had run away when she was needed most.

"Gentlemen," she continued, her voice softer, somewhat shakier, "I appreciate your trip to retrieve me, and I apologize if it has been a fruitless journey. I regret that my husband's orders are in conflict with my actions, but I am not ready to leave the house. This is not about my life," she said, pausing, and letting her eyes fill before blinking the tears away, realizing the truth of the statement only as she said it aloud. "It's about so much more than me."

"Mrs. Madison, consider your family! Consider the threat to national security if they take you hostage. We have orders, and you're acting childish, if you permit me to say so."

"Quite the opposite, sirs," she said, taking large strides to stand before them, so she could stare hard into their faces. They would never know the measures she'd already taken for national security. "This decision is one I've weighed with utmost deliberation. I resent the implication that I would ever do anything to endanger the country. And if you want to take me now, you will have to take me in chains."

The messengers slowly backed away toward the door, shaking their heads and muttering under their breath. She heard the slam of the door as they left, and the finality of their absence made the room suddenly ghostly. If only they understood this wasn't simply her being stubborn: She had to find the map!

Dolley turned back to searching, toting out a fresh box of papers from beneath the desk.

Her husband had ridden out to the troops yesterday after receiving a discouraging dispatch from Secretary of State Monroe: *The enemy are in full march to Washington. Have the materials prepared to destroy the bridges.* Now, even the colonel with his hundred men left to stand guard over Washington had evacuated, leaving only her, and her gardener, her faithful French domestic John, and a handful of slaves.

Never had Dolley felt so alone. The British were coming, a Vesper with them. Coming to destroy not only her home, but the most important American landmark in the country's short history, *the President's House,* and everything it contained. Every last possession she'd ever owned and all of the American treasures this fledgling country had worked so hard to amass. The historic home of a new nation was about to burn to the ground like a pile of firewood.

Through the silky red curtains she'd chosen when they moved in, she could see the nervous workings of people on the street as they began to pack up and depart. Smashed windows. Crushed plants. Carriage wheels across the street and screeching horses, shop doors shaken closed, whistles sounding alarm, vendors attempting to hawk last-minute deals before their businesses were destroyed. The whole district was upended.

Memories of the house flashed before her — how excited she'd been when they'd moved in, state dinners with her husband, Wednesday drawing room parties, family picnics in the gardens, important official meetings, and underneath it all, a haven for her secret Madrigal family.

A cannon sounded in the distance—Dolley froze. The battle was practically over and there were still entire wings to search, chambers and antechambers within the wings, and no one she could trust to help her find the map.

She dove back into the papers, resisting the urge to run her fingers along the mansion's beautiful gilded furniture and plush woven tapestries. She felt certain that this would be the last time she'd be in this grand space.

Smoke hissed through the Bladensburg air, and the whistle of rocket fire assaulted Captain Cyrus Ramsay's ears. This new British weapon, this rocket, was a force unforeseen. Red smoke threaded the sky above the battlefield, as if the clouds were trailing blood from gunshot wounds.

The British troops were advancing up the hill, and Ramsay dove behind the parapet against which he and his troops had dug a trench.

The battle was wearing down—it would be over soon, Ramsay knew, a complete embarrassment for him and the other outmatched American troops. Today, the president and the secretary of state had been present to witness their humiliation, which made it hurt all the worse. With this loss, it was now certain that the British would take the capital. As if to put an exclamation mark on the thought, another missile arched over Ramsay's head and exploded thirty yards in front him.

Ramsay swung around over the top of the wall and took aim at the redcoats on horseback headed his way. Through the sights of his rifle, Ramsay locked in on the British general who'd been particularly murderous earlier in the afternoon — Ramsay recognized him because this man wore his red and gold hat with the brim pulled all the way down, almost over his eyes, so that the plume tilted forward, the ridiculous plating catching glints from the sun. The general's rifle could not miss, as American soldiers strewn across the field clearly evidenced. He reloaded faster than anyone Ramsay had ever seen, and with each successful shot, a sickening smile twisted the general's face.

Ramsay took aim and fired at the tilted hat, but the general had reflexes like a cat and dodged out of the way. The bullet barely missed brushing his ears, instead whistling through the general's hat, pushing it off his forehead to reveal a hideous disfigurement.

Ramsay's hands shook as he lowered his gun. He couldn't take his eyes off the general's forehead. There, plain as day, was a deep gash slashed across his brow. The man had been cut, scarred with a letter just over his eyes, a letter that would immediately signal his true identity to any Madrigal. The scar, like a furrowed brow above his furrowed brow, was the letter V. This man was no ordinary British general. He was a Vesper, and perhaps the deadliest Vesper of them all.

Madrigals in Europe had warned of a man with a famously crooked mustache and scarred forehead, who served as a general in the British army. Among other worthy souls who'd died by his hands, a highly gifted Madrigal operative had been bested by the general in a bloody sword fight several months ago. The general had given the Madrigal operative a death blow straight to the stomach. But before the Madrigal had fallen, he'd slashed out at his opponent, scarring the general's forehead with a V so other Cahills would know him immediately for what he was.

At that moment, the general turned his head and caught Ramsay's horrified gaze. The general's brows knit together so that the V carved into his forehead grew sharper and deeper. *It looks just like devil's horns*, Ramsay thought as the general coolly looked him over. *He knows! He knows I've recognized him!*

The general slowly raised his rifle. Ramsay started sprinting. The first line of American soldiers had already fallen back in defeat, so he did not draw attention as he fled the field. But inside, Ramsay felt like a target moving on a dartboard. He had to get away from the front lines and to the President's House; he had to keep the map safe. If the general got his hands on the ring . . . Ramsay could barely handle the thought. The horror of being too late made Ramsay run even faster, his feet barely touching the ground as he ran for camp.

Ramsay rounded the bend, every step bringing him closer to the camp and closer to a horse, the fastest horse he could find. But as he raced the last ten yards and his eyes scanned the camp, Ramsay realized something was wrong. The tents were set up for sleeping and eating, the food stash and the medical supplies lay at the ready. But it was quiet, so quiet he could hear the twigs crack beneath him. There was only one person left in camp, a boy too young to fight. "Where are the others?" Ramsay yelled. "What happened to the reserves?"

"Called away to the flank," the boy answered. "There's no one left but me!"

Ramsay cursed. All the proper horses were on the battlefield behind him, or away with the reserves. The only animals left at camp were the packhorses, a scrawny collection of ill-trained beasts. Ramsay chose the best of them, a thin mare that tried to bite him as he threw a saddle on her and prepared to break for the back paths, which were overgrown with shrubbery and brush.

The early afternoon heat had set in and Ramsay could feel the distant rumble of storms building behind him. The redcoats weren't used to the punishing sun and humidity — he'd seen some on the battlefield drop to the ground from heatstroke, the Americans' lone amusement on a day that had blistered their pride. Ramsay's uniform was torn, his skin scratched and bruised and filthy from battle, but these were the least of his ills. Ramsay knew the general would be coming for him, that it would be a race to the river with death breathing down his neck. In his mind flashed the faces of his platoon members, those he'd watched die of gunshot wounds on the field, and his ears filled with the unmistakable shriek of the rockets and the path of destruction they had carved. Yes, a return to British rule would ruin the country for the rest of his lifetime, but if the Vespers took control, the *world* would never recover.

Ramsay had one foot in the stirrup when a rifle shot screamed past his ear. The horse bolted and Ramsay was lucky to hang on, his saddle sliding precariously down the mare's side. Ramsay managed to hoist himself up, only the one foot securely in the stirrup, and tried desperately to slide the other one into place as the mare galloped on. He was still out of breath from his sprint back to camp, and everything in him called out for a small sip of water. The horse's gait was lopsided as a result of the saddle, and because she had probably never gone faster than a trot in her short animal life. Her gallop rocked the unsteady saddle with each stride.

Ramsay whipped his head around and caught sight of the general behind him, reloading his rifle. Ramsay whipped his head forward again. The back roads were laced with tree roots and overturned saplings. The horse raced past the obstacles with breakneck speed, each upturned tree trunk that blocked their path nearly sending Ramsay flying from the mare's back.

The thundering of hooves sounded behind him, closing in. Ramsay leaned forward, grabbing tufts of the mare's mane, clinging to her while he urged, "Go, girl, go! Faster, faster!" into her matted ears. His heels clicked into her ribs. And, as if his words had been a magical incantation, the little mare picked up speed.

But the path was giving way before them to smaller tracks—the trees blurring into a streak of sky and woods. The vegetation grew dense and tangled; the way forward less and less clear. Thick, prickly bushes choked the path, and trees cut off the route, forcing Ramsay to ride around them.

The mare wasn't fast enough to stay ahead of the general's horse for very long. Just when Ramsay hoped he'd put some distance between them, the Vesper's mount stampeded forward.

The general's horse was so close behind him, Ramsay could practically feel its breath. He'd have to throw the general off course—even if only for a few seconds, just long enough to make a breakaway.

The branches that hung over the path were treacherous and wide, forcing Ramsay to duck down on his horse so as not to knock his head. With one hand still gripping the mane, Ramsay reached for his sword on his belt. The saddle slid on the mare's back when Ramsay shifted his weight, nearly hurling him onto the bumpy track. Ramsay clamped his knees around the mare, pushing his feet more firmly in the stirrups. Then he stood up, taking a solid whack at a thick branch above.

The branch swung down fast and hard, unloosing a flurry of smaller branches, and Ramsay dipped out of the way. Ramsay glanced over his shoulder to see the general get hit by a branch, his arms covering his head as bits of the tree rained down on him.

Chopping any branches that he could reach, Ramsay left a furious storm of twigs and leaves behind him as he rode. He hacked at boughs and anything he could reach or slash in order to block the path. He wanted to knock the general in the forehead with a thick branch, or, short of that, at least slow him down. From over his shoulder Ramsay saw General V's sword now thrashing in front of him, too, his arms flailing wildly as he tried to slash the debris crashing down on him. *Anything to keep the rifle off his shoulder,* Ramsay thought.

The sound of water gushing over rocks reached Ramsay slowly at first and then with more force. He'd reached the river.

The Potomac was wide, and the water rushed past swiftly, carrying small pieces of saplings in its current. Ramsay's mare juddered to a halt, uncertain about her willingness to cross without a bridge. Ramsay kicked her to charge through, but the mare wouldn't budge.

Ramsay kicked his heel into the mare's belly once more, but she reared up in protest. General V was approaching, his horse's hooves thundering behind them, and another gunshot exploded behind the trees. The noise gave Ramsay's mare the motivation she needed. She bolted into the water, the water swirling into Ramsay's boots.

We'll make it! thought Ramsay. *I can lose him on the other side.*

They were halfway across the river when a bullet hit Ramsay squarely in the back.

The horse, frenzied by the sound of the gunshot, jumped almost out of the water and dragged herself across. When they reached the other side, Ramsay swiveled around, his back shrieking in protest, and fired a round at the general. But his vision had blurred with the pain in his back, and the bullet hit the general's thigh, knocking him from his horse.

General V landed with a *thwack*, knocked unconscious, and his horse was startled into the river. The Hanoverian chugged across, eyes wild above the swiftly surging water. Ramsay managed to slide off the mare's back and catch the Hanoverian's reins. With a grateful pat to the mare, he mounted the Hanoverian and raced off into the forest.

Ramsay struggled now, urging the general's horse to its fastest gallop. He knew it was the last ride of his life. He would not make it to the President's House, but he could still deliver his message. There was a Madrigal house nearby, if he could only hold on that long. He was flying now, though he would have liked to have taken off his blood-soaked shirt and washed it in the river, rinsed his skin of the blood that he could feel sticking to his uniform and running down his back. He would have liked to have lain down in the water and let the currents slip over him, drink in all that his spreading thirst would take, let the river rinse his body and carry him away.

But Ramsay had a mission, even though each stride made him clench his teeth against the pain. He cut through the woods like a knife, the trees swirling before him. *Hold on*, he told himself as he fought against unconsciousness. *For the love of all things, hold on.*

The knock was insistent. It pounded and pounded and would not let up, shaking the walls around the door.

"Is someone there!?" came a strained voice from outside. Frederick had only come into the inn for a heel of bread and hunk of cheese to eat before returning to his chores in the barn. He had discovered that work was the only way to root out the thoughts creeping in about his parents—were they still alive? Would they make it home tonight?

Now the knock on the door brought Frederick up short. This was the entrance to the Warrens' personal apartments, a door used only by Frederick and his parents. Visitors went to the bar at the main inn, and only the closest of friends were invited into the Warrens' private rooms. What if, despite his parents' best assurances, the British had come to capture him after all? Or the Vespers, the people out to *extinguish* him?

Frederick searched frantically through the apartment for something to defend himself with, but there was precious little, since his father had taken the rifle this morning. As a desperate last attempt, Frederick grabbed a kitchen knife, his hands shaking as he tried to hold it steady.

"Please," the voice rasped as the rapping continued. "You must let me in. It's a matter of life and death."

The voice was commanding but hoarse, as if the speaker was finding it difficult to form each word.

Frederick froze with the knife held weakly at his side. He knew he must open the door. His parents had left. He was the man of the house now.

Slowly, he forced his feet to cross the room and pressed his hand up on the doorknob. The other hand retained the knife at his side. The afternoon heat had made the stagnant air unbearable, and already he could feel his head begin to ache and a sweat form at his temples.

"Is anyone there? Please, you must reply!" the voice cried. "I've just come from Bladensburg."

Frederick turned the handle, but he was unprepared for what he saw. He leapt back and let out a yelp before he could stop himself. An American soldier stood clutching his side, his hands and stomach covered in blood, the breath wheezing from him. "Water," the soldier said.

Frederick was too stunned to move.

"Please," the soldier insisted.

Frederick dropped the knife and raced to the pitcher on the table to pour fresh water into a tin mug. He led the soldier to a chair at the table, the same one where his family took meals, and asked if the soldier wanted some bread and cheese. This, Frederick decided, was what his parents would have offered.

"No, thank you," the solider said, as if the thought of food, and not his bleeding wound, brought him great pain. The water looked like a struggle to get down, each sip making the soldier wince, but the man continued to drink.

"Son," the soldier wheezed, "thank—you—for—kindness you've shown, but I must speak in private with the owners of inn. Where may I find them?" The soldier was resting one arm on the table, leaning heavily on it to keep his frame upright, and with the other was grasping his side to try and staunch the blood.

Frederick wondered about all of the blood; he'd never seen so much before. He swallowed to push down a tide of nausea. But his parents had always been generous to people who needed help—stragglers who wandered in off the road or poor people without homes.

"Sir, I'm sorry, they're away on business. Could I send for the doctor? You don't look well, soldier."

The soldier groaned painfully, his face turning white. He lifted a bloody hand to his forehead, streaking the dirt on his face with blood. His words were obscured by his wheezing breaths. "Too late for doctor . . . I need someone . . . who knows my or-or-orders, to relay an urgent message."

The soldier's face fell. He looked like he was going to cry, a seemingly proud man like this.

"Sir," Frederick said, wanting to sound brave, though his voice squeaked a little, "perhaps I could help?"

The soldier took stock of him between shallow breaths, his eyebrows furrowed. "You're—just—a boy. I need an agent. I need a . . ." The soldier couldn't go on.

"You need a Cahill." Frederick finished the man's sentence, sitting down at the table in the chair beside him. *Serious, for once.* His parents' words echoed in his head. "I am a Cahill. What do you need?"

The soldier just stared at him, taking breaths.

"My p-parents," Frederick stammered, needing to fill the silence while the man held his chest. "My parents are the innkeepers you seek. You already knew this, yes? That's why you're here."

"You. Son," the soldier said, raising a blood-slicked hand to point at him, "You must—carry a message to the President's House."

"Sir?"

"Take the horse that brought me. Leave immediately. And tell the master the message I give you. If you fail, the Vespers win—"

Vespers. Frederick let the sound of the word sit in the silence—it sounded like snakes and whispers, the hiss of an evil sendoff. Vespers could extinguish them. If the Vespers won, his parents were vulnerable—and what if they never came home? What if his parents were next on their list?

Frederick forced himself to nod and tried to appear calm. "Yes, sir."

The soldier rasped in more air. All of the talking had depleted him, and his breathing was noisy again. He brought the water to his lips once more, letting his hand slide off his side after he took a sip, the blood gushing freely.

Frederick didn't know how on earth he'd make good on this promise, but he found himself saying, "I'll take your message, soldier."

The soldier nodded, unable to keep his head up any longer. He folded his arms on the table and rested his head on them. With his last clear words, the soldier warned that General V, the man who had shot him, was out to destroy the President's House. Then he whispered the task that Frederick needed to complete: "The map—the map, Gideon's ring." But his speech was already becoming garbled and nonsensical. "Find it. The color of old age. Roots of our father."

Frederick asked the man what he meant, and when he didn't respond, Frederick repeated the senseless words over and over to try and make sense of what the soldier had said. *Color of old age. Roots of our father.*

Each time, the words felt stranger and stranger. What did he mean?

The soldier took a last look at him, nodded his assurance, whispered a barely audible, "God bless you, young Madrigal," and put his head down on the table for the last time. He did not lift it again.

Frederick waited a moment before disrupting the man, shaking him desperately.

"Sir," Frederick said, but the man did not stir. It was the stillest Frederick had ever seen another human being. It reminded him of when Bessie, their cow, had delivered a stillborn calf. The stillness was what had frightened him as a boy, though, of course, he'd pretended he was fine, and even tried to brag about it later to his friends, that he'd seen a dead calf and they hadn't.

"Sir!" Frederick repeated, louder now. He put his head to the man's chest, and when he heard no heartbeat, cried out in horror at what had just transpired before him. The man had died on their kitchen table. The brave soldier was gone.

Surely his parents would have known what to do, but they weren't there. Should he run down the road and call for someone to assist him? Would the soldier need to be taken to the doctor, or the church cemetery? Where was this soldier's family? Where was his own?

Frederick looked down at the soldier, *Ramsay*, a tag on his shirt read. The bullet wound! General V, Ramsay's killer, had chased him down. If the Vespers found the body, they'd know why he was at the inn and where he was going. Frederick had to move Ramsay's body.

Frederick's mind reeled. There wasn't time to think about what he was doing or to be afraid. He shut off his mind and forced his body into action. Stumbling to the back of the apartment, Frederick pulled the sheet off his bed. He slid the man off the chair and laid him gently on the floor. Then Frederick draped the sheet over the man's body and rolled Ramsay into it so he was fully wrapped. Bending down, he hoisted Ramsay up. The soldier was heavy, like the shipments of feed that arrived by cart and usually required two men to transport to the barn. Frederick dragged the soldier across the floor toward the door, the man's legs trailing beneath the sheet.

Please, please let no one see, Frederick prayed. He'd barely issued this prayer when Frederick heard the door unlatch. Amos, their servant, was standing in the doorway, there to turn down the beds, as he did every afternoon. Amos gave a start of shock and gaped at Frederick.

"Amos!" Frederick cried. "This man was in battle at Bladensburg, he stumbled in off the road. We have to move him."

"I'll send for the mayor," Amos said, his face urgent. "Leave him there until help arrives."

"Amos," Frederick implored, "this man was being chased by a British general. We can't let them know he was here. Can you help me carry him to the barn? Just until my parents return?"

Amos looked too alarmed to speak.

"We can't endanger the inn, not with the British so close!" A dead soldier in his arms would put his home at risk—how had this happened in the course of an afternoon cheese break?! Frederick was having trouble connecting his thoughts.

Amos nodded silently, still stunned. Then he kicked into gear. Amos lifted the soldier's legs while Frederick gripped the arms, which were growing heavier by the second. Slowly they backed through the door and down the stairs one by one. They couldn't risk catching the attention of the other workers at the inn, and they especially could not afford to upset the patrons. And what if the Vespers were watching them?

Frederick and Amos were in plain view now, needing to cross the green to the barnyard as fast as possible without anyone seeing them.

In the barn, Frederick laid Ramsay on a bed of hay. Blood had seeped through the sheet, so they laid a vegetable tarp over the body. Amos filled a pail of soapy water to scrub the path of blood. He promised that he'd find the mayor after he was finished. The servant crossed himself as he passed the body lying outstretched on the hay.

Frederick was terrified. This Madrigal agent had died right in front of him, and his family was in the same mortal danger. If he failed to deliver Ramsay's message, their fate could be the same as the soldier's.

Frederick knelt down before the dead soldier and prayed in earnest for the first time in his life. He'd been to church before. Every Sunday, in fact, but he usually prayed for his friends to fall for one of his tricks or for the pretty girls in the square to dance with him during the May Day festivals. But on this day, Frederick prayed with everything he had to beat the Vespers and to keep his family safe. He prayed for the future of his troubled nation. Finally, Frederick wished this soldier, this *Ramsay*, a restful peace in heaven above.

God, watch over me now, as I continue this dead man's journey.

The soldier's horse clopped its way east toward the capital, Frederick riding uneasily. He'd had to adjust the stirrups, since Ramsay had been so much taller, but he still felt unfit to ride such a mammoth animal, and his heart clapped loudly in his rib cage.

As a twelve-year-old boy on this enormous black cavalry horse, Frederick drew looks from the local villagers, some of whom knew him. A few heckled or hooted or called up that he should not be playing pranks with other people's horses.

Frederick pretended not to hear them and ushered the fine large horse along. For once, this wasn't a prank, and he wasn't being irresponsible. *Serious, for once.*

The road was windy, and the skies were darkening, a storm blowing through soon. The air held the wet smoky smell of early fall. Up ahead, Frederick saw a group of American soldiers in the village square, watering their horses from a pump by the communal well.

Sweaty and bearded, some of the men were still wearing their caps, while others hung their heads. The square around them was quieter than it should have been, the way it got before a riot, or a revered politician's speech. Even the local tavern was muted. Some of the town families approached the soldiers to offer their thanks and appreciation in hushed tones. They served up plates of food, and gently tried to coax out what had happened at Bladensburg.

Frederick could tell that it had been a rough fight. Gunpowder coated the soldiers' brows, their uniforms were ripped, skin scratched. Sweat soaked through the heavy cloth and their faces were splotchy with heat fatigue. The men, quite simply, looked beaten.

Their expressions darkened at the sight of Frederick, and they began shouting and pointing at him. The horse whinnied and whined, the soldiers storming toward him with death in their eyes.

As Frederick approached, the soldiers began to throw things at him, rocks and heavy branches.

"Redcoat!" one of the men yelled at Frederick, coming at him fast and hard.

What was he talking about?!

"Bloody traitor!" screamed another. Frederick tried to ride faster, as this horse was the fleetest he'd ever ridden. But why were they screaming at him? Just as he thought he'd safely made it out of the village, Frederick saw two men on horseback coming after him down the path.

Frederick kicked his horse, urging her onward, gripping the reins and holding on as tightly as he could.

Just get me to Washington. To Washington! Frederick repeated to himself. The men behind him jeered. They were calling things to him: "Run, coward!" "If you ever show your face again . . ."

Frederick believed he was safely out of eyeshot and that the men would leave him alone now. But just as he was relaxing into his saddle, the horse stumbled and Frederick fell to the ground.

His back took the most shock from his fall. Frederick lay still, waiting for feeling to return to his legs.

From above his head, Frederick heard a voice say, "You some kind of Tory errand boy, traitor?"

Frederick groaned as the feeling began to return to his side—the speed with which his body had been thrown made the ground that much harder when he'd hit it, like he'd been kicked in the kidney.

"Sir, why do you keep calling me that? I am as American as you are," Frederick moaned.

"If you're not a British errand boy, then what are you doing on a British horse?"

From his immobile position on the ground, Frederick's face flushed. Of course! Ramsay must have stolen it. How could he not have realized and tried to remove the cloth regalia the horse was brandishing? It was the colors—red, gold, and black. He might as well have been waving a British flag and singing "Rule, Britannia!"

From the ground, Frederick managed a grin before standing up and brushing himself off. "Why, stealing it, of course."

With the horse stripped of her enemy uniform, the ride was much smoother. Churches and schools and stores dotted the greens. The trees were less dense as more of the land was razed and parceled into lots for farming than the roads down which Frederick had come.

Wooden cabins lined the roads, set back behind fenced yards that would normally keep the animals in, though now most of the animals had been herded away. Wheat and tobacco fields spread out around him, the corn getting taller than Frederick, anticipating harvest.

Frederick could see the town approaching. In the distance lay all of the government offices. The great strip of green, the Mall, was coming into view. At the outset, everything looked peaceful.

But the closer he drew to the President's House,

the clearer it became that the city was about to be attacked. Everyone was packing up and evacuating as fast as they could, riding the opposite direction as Frederick. Farther in, the roads were clogged with carriages of families, mothers holding babies, coaches packed to the very last inch with trunks and tools, animals and food, a chair or table, if it could be carted off. Everywhere, the sounds of pandemonium rang out.

Men were yelling, women shrieking, babies crying, children squabbling, dogs barking, chickens squawking, horses whinnying, as if even the animals could tell there might not be a tomorrow. The pre-storm wind picked up stray garbage and whipped pieces around and around, like a wild carousel. Abandoned goats loitered in the road.

As Frederick got deeper into the city, the roads emptied out, and an eerie quiet filled the air. People had abandoned everything. Windows and doors were left haphazardly open, fences were unlatched, and Frederick saw cows lazing on the side of the street.

Frederick could hear windows breaking — he suspected people were taking advantage of the opportunity to vandalize as much property as they could before fleeing the city.

The Potomac ran alongside him, helping Frederick orient himself as he raced toward an empty Pennsylvania Avenue. The river was brown with silt and mud, and the sky had grayed over. The humidity hung thick in the air. Mosquitoes were everywhere, and Frederick had to wave his hand in front of his face to keep the gnats away. Washington had been built on a swamp, and Frederick had never felt this as strongly as he did now. He mopped his brow with a worn handkerchief.

At 1600 Pennsylvania Avenue, Frederick paused for a moment to take in the President's House. It was a breathtaking sight. Even in its final hours, with the British on their way to sack it, the house stood proudly. The three floors and eleven bays were shimmering in the daylight, along with the columns and the trees that horseshoed around them. The windows were tall and seemingly endless, and a parapet bordered the roof like icing around the edges of a frosty, lonely white cake.

Once again, Ramsay's words rattled through Frederick's brain. *If you fail, the Vespers win.* The sky clouded over, losing light, and the wind was rustling up in the trees like a soft-shoed burglar. He had to tell the president that General V was at large, and he had to find that map. If he didn't, his family might share the same fate as this beautiful house.

The President's House gardens looked deserted. Roundabouts led to orchards, and flower beds flanked the walking paths, leading to copses of fruit trees and vegetable gardens. The rosebushes were releasing the last of their fragrant smell from the summer's final dying blossoms. Fountains, statues, and birdbaths broke the carpet of green. Acres of trees were divided into plots, and shady pavilions offered solace from the sun. Ivy grew up the portico's trellises that gave way to the famous mansion.

Frederick had worried that it would be difficult to get into the house, but entry now appeared to be almost too easy. He'd expected to have to slip past rows and rows of uniformed guards bearing rifles, then to have to fight off servants and state officials, but there was almost no one around. The only people he had seen had been two slaves, surveying the empty city in alarm.

The wrought-iron gate was locked—*no surprise,* but Frederick was a good climber from lazy summers spent in the trees around the inn. He made short order of the fence and hopped down with a thud onto the lawn. He checked both ways—still clear.

A lone guard—or was it a servant?—stepped out onto the portico. Frederick lurched to take cover behind the hedges, but he'd been seen.

"You there!" the man cried. "Out!"

Frederick scampered across the emerald lawn, his feet almost sliding out from under him on the freshly cut grass. The man charged after him, waving a shovel. He was wearing coveralls and thick boots. Frederick was running from the president's gardener.

Frederick bounded toward the corner of the house, but the gardener was gaining on him. He swung the shovel out at Frederick, but Frederick dodged it by a millimeter's breadth.

Frederick feinted one direction and at the last second turned the corner. He scanned the grounds for anywhere he might hide from the gardener, but everything was visible. He was about to make a break for the orchards, somewhere to take cover when—could it be?

An open window on the far side of the house.

Frederick sprinted to the siding and threw himself through the opening. He crashed onto the floor and froze for a moment before righting himself. He slammed shut the glass, locking the top. Frederick found himself suddenly in the cool drawing room of the President's House—without a clue as to how he would now find the president.

The entrance hall alone was bigger than Frederick's family's entire apartment. It was all far too spectacular a sight on such a terrible day—even the air felt more majestic beneath the marbled ceilings. Frederick would have liked to have stopped and admired each individual nook and cranny. But none of it would survive come nightfall. And if he wasn't careful, neither would he.

Frederick bolted from room to room, checking over his shoulder in case the gardener returned. He ducked behind columns and dove behind furniture, but no one was there. The space was deserted, and the president was nowhere to be found. The entrance hall led to a cross hall, with what appeared to be a state dining room on one side, and a smaller, private dining room on the other. Objects and historical artifacts were displayed artfully on the floor-to-ceiling shelves, and white wainscot ran the length of the floors.

The president's library looked as if a storm had blown through it. Papers were scattered everywhere.

Was anyone home?

Frederick heard footsteps and leapt beneath a desk. The library was covered in plush oriental rugs and smelled like cedars and tobacco. After a few seconds passed, he tiptoed out.

It was the gardener again, in a hurry. Frederick followed him to the marble staircase. He had to take two steps at a time to keep up, then fall back far enough that the man wouldn't see him. The stairwell unfolded into more enormous rooms.

Frederick trailed the gardener through another central hall, then a lavish sitting room and a handsome antechamber that unfurled into a drawing room. The softly lit lamps, complete sets of sparkling crystal, and intricate rugs beneath their feet — the British would make mincemeat of all of it in no time. Where was the president?

Frederick noted how the wallpaper changed from mint green to powder blue to a blush pink, and now the walls shimmered coral and gold. They'd reached the first lady's wing. Through an arched entrance, he spied a salon that boasted a view of the street.

Down the hall, Frederick could hear metal clattering to the floor. The voice of the gardener came through brusquely. Frederick pressed his ear to the door. Could he hear the president's voice inside, too?

The door opened sharply, and Frederick stumbled to the floor of what appeared to be the silver room. Cased in glass, the famed silver made even the shadows glimmer. Frederick cowered on the floor, the crystal cabinets showering prisms of light onto the gardener and the woman standing beside him, the first lady.

Frederick recognized Dolley Madison from lithographs in the papers. She was wearing a pink lace frock and her face was made up. Frederick was suddenly aware of his muddied knees. With her large rings and white ruffled cap, not even a British invasion could hamper this lady's style. Even with her life on the line, Dolley Madison was dressed for the victory party.

But she was not about to pause for admiration.

"Well," Dolley exclaimed, "so this is the vagrant from the garden." Turning to the gardener, she said, "I'll handle this. I need you to return to the watch, and thank you for the updates."

"You s-s-see . . . ," Frederick stammered. He'd been expecting the president, and he found himself slightly tongue-tied in the presence of such beauty.

Some of the crystal cases gaped open where contents had been removed, as if the President's House had already been burglarized. At the center of the silver room, a large leather trunk sat open on the table. The plates and goblets and platters missing from the room's cases were carefully arranged inside it.

"Are you just going to stand there?" Dolley asked him. "Speak! State your purpose."

"Ma'am, I must speak with your husband at once," Frederick said, regaining his voice. "I come with urgent news."

"My husband has left, as has everyone who serves the president. Any news you have should be directed to me. Are you here with an estimated time of the British arrival? My gardener was just on the roof and spotted them in the distance—we have one hour."

Frederick felt his face and shoulders drop—all of this work. Here he was, actually *in* the President's House, but the president was not even there to take the news he'd traveled so far to deliver. But if he failed . . .

Dolley returned to packing her silver. There was one last crystal cabinet to be unloaded, its glass door edged in gold. With the speed of five people, she inspected the silver pieces, wrapped them in cheesecloth, and deposited them into the leather trunk.

"Madam First Lady," Frederick began.

"Dolley," Dolley said. "And if you're going to stay, you may as well be of some use. I need you to help me pack the contents of this console. I'd sooner die than let those redcoats see as much as one ounce of this silver."

Frederick began moving pieces, though he was

slower than she was. His hands had never cupped such wealth, and he was afraid he would break something. The silver felt cool to the touch, and Frederick thought this is what lakes would feel like if they could be magically solidified.

"If you see any strange markings on them, please show me," Dolley said.

Frederick cleared his throat and opened his mouth to speak.

"Yes, yes, out with it," she cried. "There's a war approaching, or haven't you heard?"

"I'm from a village outside the district, near—near Bladensburg," Frederick sputtered. "A s-soldier came to our door today while my parents were out. He died on our kitchen table, but he had a message for the president, about, er, secret affairs."

"What kind of secret affairs?" Dolley asked without taking her eyes off the silver, crossing the room in what looked like three strides back to the trunk.

Frederick took a breath before taking the big leap. "He spoke to me about what your husband will understand to be a classified Cahill matter."

Dolley gasped. She'd finally stopped moving.

"Are *you* aware of these matters?" Frederick asked, unsure whom he was allowed to speak with about Madrigal affairs. "I really must get word to your husband."

"*I* am the Cahill," Dolley whispered, though there was no one around to hear. "It is *I* to whom your message should be directed. James has no idea — and if word ever gets to him . . ."

"You?" Frederick exclaimed.

"How do I know you're not a spy?" Dolley cried. "You haven't even properly introduced yourself."

"My name is Frederick Warren, madam, an honor to make your acquaintance," Frederick declared. No turning back now — Ramsay's message! "There is a dangerous man disguised as a British operative headed this way. General W."

Dolley looked at him as if he were crazy, before her face paled as white as the house they were in. "General V, you mean." Dolley gasped, one hand rising to her throat. "I have to find the map!"

"The messenger was not making sense when he died," Frederick explained, recounting the words Ramsay had moaned on his deathbed about the map and Gideon's ring. "'The color of old age. The roots of our father.'"

Dolley sank into a chair without seeming to realize that she'd been standing. "The map to Gideon's ring. The map is hidden in this house, somewhere. Not even I know where it is. General V can't be allowed to find it — if he does, the Vespers will rise to power, and we'll never know freedom again."

After so much motion, her stillness signaled despair like none other Frederick had seen. He thought of his mother that morning, clutching him close.

Shouldn't he make a break for home, as fast as he

could, to keep himself safe? He recalled the promise he'd made to his mother — that he would run at the first sign of the British.

Technically, his job here was finished. Frederick could leave knowing that he delivered Ramsay's message, and the mission was complete. But if the Vespers won, they would strike down Madrigal agents, and his family would never be safe. They'd always be hunted, and they could all end up like Ramsay.

His parents were vulnerable right now. They'd left him for Madrigal business. What if they were falling into a killer's trap?

Frederick's mission was only just beginning.

"The British are forty-five minutes out, madam," the gardener called.

If they stayed here, it could mean their lives. If they left, the Vespers could find the hidden map and uncover Gideon's ring. It was so awful Frederick almost laughed. The way that horror, when pressed too close, can look funny.

"Well . . . ," Frederick said, jolted from his nightmare. Except the nightmare was ongoing, and he was wide-awake. "We should search another room, as this one is just about finished. What's the most valuable thing you have left?" Frederick asked.

He looked at the first lady directly for the first time, across the table. They were in it together now.

Dolley hadn't spoken for a while, but she responded without even thinking now. "General Washington's portrait in the state dining room. I couldn't possibly leave until it's secured," Dolley said.

"Forty-four minutes," the gardener called, bustling through the halls. They hauled the trunk packed with most of the room's contents down with gardener, to be sent away for safekeeping with the others. The rest of the silver they would try to return for in what little time they had left.

Downstairs, the portrait shone like a beacon in the dining room. The long table gleamed with polish, and the chairs stood proudly beside it, like a row of soldiers waiting at attention.

The oil on canvas depicted a regal Washington holding a sword in one hand and stretching his other arm magnanimously outward, his palm upturned. The president was dressed in a rich black coat and leggings, a red velvet chair behind him and an inkwell and quill at his side. The colors were vivid and majestic, the reds plush and soft-looking, the likeness of his face so real it felt that the man might walk out of the painting at any moment. His face, in fact, possessed a glow, his eyes that lifelike sparkle.

Before Frederick could speak, the first lady's eyes filled up with tears. With all of the Vesper threats, Frederick had forgotten all that Dolley was losing at the hands of the British, too. This country that had fought proudly, this house that stood as a testament to independence. Now to be dismantled by the British they'd once defeated.

Frederick worried about her — a crack was surfacing in her polished veneer.

"Do you think it's possible —" Frederick ventured.

"Silver is the color of old age," Dolley began, allowing some of her optimism to return to her voice, and they looked up at America's first president, with his distinguished gray wig.

"Roots of our father," Frederick continued. "Father, as in father of the country!"

"But there's no map on it!" Dolley cried.

"No map that we can *see*," Frederick corrected. "Let's remove the portrait, and then we can really inspect it. I think this has to be it, right?!" Frederick could feel the hope building inside him, as if hope alone could make something true. "The frame looks heavy."

"The frame is not important," Dolley said, her cheeks flushing with fresh and hurried excitement. "Only the painting matters. We need to make haste if we're going to get it out of the building."

Frederick scanned the room for something that would break the wood. As fast as he could, he sprinted back the way he had come toward the garden, through doomed room upon room.

In the garden, Frederick found a wooden-handled ax near the gardener's shed. The ax's head shone brightly in the sun. The surface of the metal was scratched up, and markings crisscrossed its surface. The British would be just outside the city now.

It was almost dark, and the temperature was still

beastly, but Frederick was scarcely outside long enough to break a sweat before dashing back through the wide halls of the President's House. Frederick tried to retrace his steps so as not to lose himself in the grand maze.

Back in the dining room, Frederick let his momentum carry him up to the painting, and when Dolley nodded, he took a swing at the wooden frame, careful not to miss and hit the painting instead. The frame was gilded with gold flakes, the wood intricately engraved. It looked heavy and sturdy on the wall.

He missed the wood altogether, swinging around in a circle. Embarrassingly, the only thing the ax hit was air.

Dolley covered her mouth to stifle a laugh, and then nodded at him urgently to try again.

Frederick lined up in front of the painting, pulled his arms back, and took a hard long swing, never taking his eyes off the frame as he swung his arm around.

WHACK.

A satisfying sound, he'd hit the sweet spot of the wood. Standing back to look at his work, Frederick saw that the frame was split in a corner, cleaved in two.

The first lady cheered. "Don't worry, Frederick, I won't tell the guards. We'll tell everyone French John did it," she said, and began to gingerly peel out the still beautifully intact painting from the shattered frame. This symbol of the republic, the first president—saved only minutes before the British defaced it.

As she pulled the rest of the canvas from its

backing, the wood fell away from its hold on the wall. They held the painting at each end, as if it were a sacred scroll. George Washington stared up at them, his wig brushed and powdered. His painted face half-smiled approvingly. Father of the country, of course!

"Color of old age, roots of our father," Frederick whispered, like the words to an enchanted spell. "This is it!"

Frederick and Dolley had only taken a moment to search the painting, their backs to the door, when they heard someone behind them.

"We'll take that for you," came a grizzled voice with a clipped British accent.

Dolley and Frederick swung around. It was General V, glowering from the entrance to the dining room. His scar scowled at them from his forehead.

Oh, no, it's actually him! Frederick could only manage one thought: escape.

General V was still in British uniform, and everything about him was long and thin, pointy as a dagger. His body looked painfully stretched, and he sported a thin crooked mustache. He had a gun pointed straight at Dolley's heart.

"Mrs. Madison," he purred, advancing toward her, "I don't believe we've met." His smile grew more twisted with each step.

Dolley trembled as he neared, the room growing smaller around her. "The British army? You're here?"

"Only our Vesper riders, my dear. The rest of the army is expected" — and here he leaned close to

Dolley's face, pausing for emphasis—"presently."

Dolley reached back and slapped his cheek, hard, defiance wrinkling her forehead.

Frederick braced himself, his heart racing uncontrollably.

Gun in hand, the general raised his arm to strike her back.

Without thinking, Frederick inserted himself between them, and fast.

The general appraised Frederick, arm still raised. "And who would you be, *boy*?" he asked, circling around both of them, as if they were lions in the circus and he was the ringmaster.

"Frederick Warren," Frederick trembled, unable to come up with a false name on the spot.

"Of Henry and Wilhelmina Warren?" General V asked.

Frederick felt like the wind had been knocked out of him. A wave of nausea almost brought him to the floor. This horrible man knew his parents by name!

"I don't know whom you mean, General," Frederick said, though General V had seen him flinch. What would he do to Frederick's parents now? Everything was Frederick's fault!

General V would not be ruffled. He turned to Dolley and repeated, " 'Color of old age,' what was it you said? 'Roots of our father'? A good one, the Vesper leadership appreciates the pains you've taken to deliver the map."

Chuckling lightly, General V said, "I'll take that

from you." With his long, spidery fingers, he reached for the canvas that Dolley clutched close to her heart. "And you will learn that no good deed," he said, taking the painting, "goes unpunished."

The basement of the President's House was a pitch-black maze. There were no windows, and Dolley and Frederick couldn't see anything. General V had forced them down the stairs and tied them to a beam in the cellar. The rope dug into their wrists and fingers. Precious seconds were racing by, and Frederick guessed the British army had just crossed the Mall.

"What do we do?" Dolley whispered.

Frederick could feel blood dripping from his knees and elbows in the darkness. He'd taken the fall down the stairs hard. It could be worse, Frederick reminded himself, thinking of Ramsay's back. *Just skinned knees.*

"The painting—the map must be hidden somewhere on it, and now it's gone! General V will know where the ring is!" Frederick whispered.

"I don't want to die here, Frederick," Dolley said. Her voice was hoarse and low.

"We won't," Frederick said, though he was shaking, trying to convince himself. "We won't," he repeated. Would General V torture them next? Would he and Dolley get caught in the flames when the British burned the house? Frederick's mind reeled.

"How can we get ourselves out of here?" Frederick ventured, more thinking aloud than actually expecting an answer.

Something crashed on the floor above them that sounded like shattered glass. Heavy footsteps pounded down the stairs.

The door creaked open, and in the blackness, Dolley and Frederick could only see a white light floating toward them, and the sound of seething breaths, rasping closer to where they were tied.

A lantern—the flame rose higher, and the shape of the general's sharpened cheekbones emerged from the darkness.

"You two!" he screeched. The lantern highlighted the shadows under his eyes and his cruel, twisting mouth. "You lied to me! And now you will *pay*!"

"What are you talking about?" Dolley cried. "You have the map!"

"Oh, you mean that hideous *painting*," he said, spit flying from his mouth. Frederick could feel her shrinking behind him in the darkness. "There was no map on that saccharine piece of child's art!"

"But—" Dolley cried, "the color of—"

Frederick nudged her to stop talking.

"Yes?" General V shrieked. "What of it?! There must be something else that answers the same riddles. And you two are going to solve it. If you don't, I am going to enjoy letting you burn.

"My only sadness is that I myself won't be here to

see it! Maybe I'll secure a good seat from just outside the grounds," he said as his voice jumped a register, delighted with himself. "Now, tell me where the map is, or the fun will *really* heat up." General V's mirth fed off Dolley's fear like smoke on cinders.

Dolley began to cry softly, and it sounded to Frederick like she was giving up. They should have fled the President's House when everyone warned that the British were close by.

Frederick couldn't think straight. How were they supposed to tell General V where the map was hidden if they didn't know themselves? Frederick's eyes searched for hints, but all he saw was blackness. They had to get out of this basement. That was the first thing.

Frederick snapped. "I'll tell you where the map is on one condition. If you let us go." Frederick's voice was clear, piercing the darkness. The wicked laughter stopped.

"Frederick," Dolley began, but he gently gripped her arm. *I'll get us out of here.*

"Mrs. Madison doesn't know where it is," Frederick corrected. *"I've* known all along. The first lady would be far too vulnerable with this type of privileged information. I was just waiting for her to leave so I could obtain it for myself — until you came in."

"And a twelve-year-old boy wouldn't be too vulnerable with intelligence of this kind? How could you possibly know such secrets?"

Frederick balked. "I have my sources." Rushing

forward, he continued, "I've seen enough of you to know better than to try and trick you now."

Frederick guessed that flattery might work, at least for the moment. "Let us leave with the portrait," Frederick added, "and I will deliver you your map."

"Frederick?!" Dolley cried. Frederick knew she must be wondering if he'd been lying to her the whole time. Or if he was now saving their lives. Or both.

"Of course," the general said, stroking his mustache, "show me the map, and I will, with certainty . . . release you."

Frederick didn't believe him for a minute. General V would probably rather die than let two Cahills walk free. But at least if they made it upstairs, they could *see.* And it bought them one step closer to escape.

General V dragged Dolley and Frederick back up the stairs toward the entrance hall. Their wrists ached from the tightly bound ropes, and it was so black they could barely see the arms pulling them up the stairs. The steps creaked as they climbed, and with each step Frederick was more determined—how to escape?

At the top of the stairs, General V pushed his captives roughly to the floor. The chandeliers shone brightly—someone must have lit the oil—and the glare blinded Dolley and Frederick, who shielded their eyes with their elbows.

"Now, where is the map?" General V roared, yanking Frederick up by the arm and swinging him around so that the general's ugly face was too close to Frederick's.

The brave slaves who'd stayed looked on in horror from the edges of the entrance hall. The French servant had left, and the gardener stood guard outdoors, ready to bolt at the last second. The slaves were the only ones left.

"Well," Frederick stammered, "you see, I have to show it to you. I can't tell you here, with so many people around."

How to buy more time?

"And, I, uh, need to see the painting, as proof that you're as good as your word."

General V flashed the knife from his belt and thrust it against Frederick's back. It did not break his skin, but the blade pierced through Frederick's shirt, so the metal pointed sharply against his skin. "Don't move, do you understand?"

Frederick nodded.

General V called for his assistants, but evidently they were already scouring the house for the map.

"Wait here," General V said, stewing with impatience.

When he left the entrance hall, Frederick turned to Dolley. "We have to run, now, let's go!"

"What about the map?" Dolley asked. They'd already started running. Their wrists and fingers were still tied together, and it slowed them.

"He doesn't know where it is—and neither do we. It will burn with the rest of the house as soon as the British arrive, and that way nobody gets it," Frederick whispered.

"We can't go out the door, there are Vespers here guarding the door."

"Maybe a back window!" Frederick cried as they raced to the side of the room where Frederick let himself in.

Frederick had locked the window after he'd landed, and there was nothing close by to break the glass. He couldn't lift much with his fingers and wrists bound.

"Quick," Dolley cried, "before General V gets back!"

Frederick raised his elbow and squeezed shut his eyes. *One, two, on three!*

SMASH.

Frederick struck the window as hard as he could. The sound of the glass shattering was the best thing he'd heard all day, and he could see the hole where his elbow had punched through. He didn't even mind the blood. His elbow hurt, but that was nothing compared to what General V would do. He hoped General V hadn't heard the crash.

"Dolley, you first," Frederick said, helping her out the window as best he could.

Dolley stuck one leg through and then the other, careful not to let the glass cut her on her way out. Slowly, she lowered herself out of the window and onto the grass outside.

Frederick got an idea. With the ragged edges still attached to the sill, Frederick rubbed the rope that bound his wrists against the sharp glass still left in the window. The first pass did nothing to the rope, and on the second pass, it barely frayed.

"Frederick!" Dolley cried from outside, "Hurry! We have to get out of here!"

Frederick could feel the rope beginning to give and the individual strands starting to unravel. He was almost there, he just had to make sure he didn't nick himself.

"There!" Frederick announced, wiggling his fingers, "I got it!"

"Bravo," came the general's voice, breathing in his ear. Two false claps followed.

Frederick dove for the window, but it was too late.

General V dropped the painting and caught Frederick around the waist, squeezing Frederick's arms behind his back.

"Run, Dolley!" Frederick yelled, and for a split second, General V released hold of Frederick's arms to catch a glimpse of Dolley on the lawn outside.

"Frederick!" Dolley cried.

In that second Frederick managed to grab the historic painting from where General V had dropped it on the floor and throw it out the window.

"The painting, Dolley!" Frederick cried. "Run for your life!"

"Frederick!" she cried. "I'll go find help!"

"Detain that woman!" General V shouted through the window. "And grab that painting!"

Frederick could hear a mad rush of footsteps chasing after Dolley.

"Take me to the map! I've had enough of you!" General V shouted into Frederick's ear, shaking him.

Frederick wracked his mind for anything that could save him. He held on to the hope that he could still solve the riddle of the map before the British set fire to the house. He just had to think of something to throw the general off the scent.

"Well, boy?" General V yelled over the chaos outside, the veins in his neck pulsing as he pressed the dagger against Frederick's jugular, just shy of breaking the skin. "You decide—the map or your life."

"It's—it's in the dining room, where you found us!" Frederick stammered. "I have to show you where."

"Well, go then, before it's destroyed!" General V shouted, his voice only barely audible over the wreckage surging in from outside.

With the knife to his neck, Frederick led General V back to the gallery, the last place he'd seen before being thrown in the basement. Maybe the last place he would see alive. Was this his death march? He took slow steps, letting his mind work itself into a frenzy, the general pushing him forward to try and rush him. But Frederick needed every second of time left.

At that moment, a sound flooded the entrance hall, echoing off the high ceiling and through the great halls. In marched the British army, in lines of two and three, bearing torches and rifles and bags for looting.

They were there to retaliate for America burning the Canadian capital, earlier in the war, and Frederick heard the glee in the voices of the enemy soldiers ready to deliver a fatal blow to the President's House. They were there to wreak real and symbolic destruction to what they still thought of as their American colony.

"God save the king! England forever!" they shouted.

In their bloodred uniforms they flooded through the pristine rooms of the President's House like fire ants, kicking over furniture, smashing crystal, shattering windows with the butts of their rifles. In short order, they tore down the red silk and velvet drapes and swept clean the carefully arranged objects from on the shelves. From the rooms above, Frederick could hear chests being broken open, mattresses sliced through. He could imagine the feathers mushrooming up into clouds. The redcoats slashed the faces of portraits on the walls — the rips slicing like scalpels through flesh.

Troops rushed past into the kitchen and dining room, raiding the cupboards. They gorged themselves on what would have been the first lady's dinner, laughing the whole time. Then they smashed the plateware and kicked over the table.

Clearly delighted by the chaos, General V pushed Frederick forward with the blade of his knife.

They were back in the dining room, and Frederick's moment was up.

"Now!" General V shouted.

Frederick frantically scanned the gallery. The other paintings had all been lifted off the sandstone walls, their shapes still outlined like ghostly shadows of what had hung before. Shredded canvas lay in piles on the floor. The dining table had been chopped into what may as well have been a pile of firewood, with the gardener's ax resting on top.

"There!" Frederick pointed, his body rushing toward the ax. This last gasp of an idea wasn't even fully formed, but Frederick had to go with it. He bent down to lift the ax by the handle. The crosshatched lines of the metal axhead, by some stroke of luck, looked almost organized, like they'd been inscribed there on purpose.

"This axhead. Here is the map," Frederick sputtered, handing it over to the general's spindly fingers. "Do you see how the lines are intersecting, that one dent in the corner—there you will find Gideon's ring."

Frederick squeezed shut his eyes as the madness escalated around them. The troops were at fever pitch now, ready to torch the place down. He awaited the final blow by General V, the certain and swift hit when his lie was discovered. Why exactly had Frederick just offered up a weapon to this maniacal killer?

Surrounded by the entire British army, the world stopped, and everything went silent. It was as if he and General V were in the room alone. Finally, Frederick opened one eye.

"Color of old age . . ." General V repeated to himself, turning the silver ax over and over in his arms, "roots of our father — the cherry trees in the garden, of course, you stupid Americans with your heritage ridiculousness."

Please, please, Frederick prayed, *let him believe this is the map. Then at least if we can't find it, the Vespers won't, either, and it will burn tonight along with the rest of the house.*

"It's a map of a cemetery in Baltimore," Frederick lied. "There's soon to be a battle there. Perhaps if you arrive before them, the ring will be yours."

Frederick hoped he sounded believable. He tried to make his voice sound as defeated as possible. "The soldier was on his way to Baltimore next, before you shot him in battle this morning."

"Your *sources,* of course," General V concluded. He kept the ax close, a grin creeping onto his face. "Well, good work, my boy. I must take leave of you now. Unfortunately, you'll have to burn with the house. It would be no good to have you out in the world — you've seen too much of me already."

Frederick ran for the door, but General V threw him against the broken bookshelf. "Pity you didn't join Mrs. Madison."

With a flourish of red and gold and black, General V was out the door, an ominous click behind him.

Frederick tried the knob and rattled the door, but it was locked tight. He ran to the window, but he was on the second floor now, and the British were guarding the property. He screamed uselessly. The noise from the British drowned out everything, and there was no one left to help him anyway.

Frederick found a nail still tacked in the wall where the painting had been. Maybe he could pick the lock!

He slid the nail through the keyhole and tried to turn it, but it was useless.

Then he ran back for a chunk of wood, and tapped the nail with it, to try and bump the lock out of its socket. The bump loosened something. Frederick jiggled the nail a few more times where the key should have gone.

Miraculously, the nail turned, and the lock tumbled back. Frederick took off down the hall as fast as he could toward the stairwell.

Frederick barely had time to process that he was still alive before he saw the kiss of flame on the walls below. In every room, the soldiers had set torches to anything they could find, and the heat that rose up was already scorching. Smoke filled the air in gray clouds; the smell of singed wood was everywhere. Frederick could hear the last of the slaves screaming outside.

Frederick made a break for the main door — maybe he could slip out without calling attention to himself. But as he was heading for the door, Frederick thought of something.

Color of old age, roots of our father. The pieces were coming together. Color of old age — "*silver is the color of old age,*" Dolley had said. Silver — he'd found Dolley in the silver room—maybe there was still time to find the map!

Frederick flew up the marble stairs, his mind racing ahead. The floors were hot beneath him, but he willed them to hold up for a few moments more, just until he found the map. *Please let there be time.*

Back in the silver room, Frederick searched furiously. The last console Dolley had left unpacked was ravaged, and there was nothing left inside.

Please, please. The heat was pressing close and the air was like an oven, but Frederick knew he was onto something. Sweat flowed off his body. Smoke swam through the room and burned his eyes.

Just one last silver piece.

Frederick ran along the edges of the room, lifting up shreds of rugs, kicking through rubble and upturning chairs. Finally, he was back at the console, where he'd first found Dolley nervously packing.

He lifted up its legs—there was a secret trapdoor in the floor! Was Frederick imagining this? Had he lost his mind? He lifted the door and found a wooden compartment. And there, in a small hatbox, was a gleaming silver urn wrapped in paper. Frederick dropped to his knees to examine it.

Engraved across its base were the words *Roots of our father.*

Inside its polished silver bowl was one letter: M.

On its base, Frederick found, at last, the real map to Gideon's ring.

Clutching the urn to his chest, Frederick raced toward the doorway. He had to fight back the smoke. The doorway was framed in fire where the wooden beams had once stood. The smoke was blinding, and tears streamed down his face, but he pushed through the black fumes that burned his eyes and nose. His whole face felt like it was melting. With his eyes closed, he grasped about for the railing of the marble stairs, taking each step as fast as he could, stumbling down with the rail as his only guide.

When he heard a crash behind him, Frederick whipped around and saw that the ceiling above him had crumbled to the ground, sending down sparks and beams flying from the flaming rafters. Frederick felt the shock of his realization: *If I'd waited a second longer upstairs, I'd be dead now.*

A flaming ceiling beam sliced down through the air, dangerously close to Frederick's face. It landed in front of him—the fire licking around the floors, up the walls. How could he get to the next room with a flaming beam blocking his path?

Frederick tried ducking beneath the beam, but the flames were too hot. The windows were burning, too, no hope of jumping out now. He was the last one left in the President's House. But would he also be the last one *out*?

Knowing this was his last chance, Frederick ran

straight toward the beam. He kicked as hard as he could, watching the sole of his shoe catch flame as it slammed into the wood in front of him.

The beam fell to the floor, spreading fire to the rugs, and Frederick leapt over them as he would a puddle. His boot was on fire now, his foot burning. Still clutching the urn with one hand, Frederick bent down and unlaced the fiery shoe, throwing it as far as possible. He raced for the exit.

The door to the outside was too hot to touch. Frederick looked around for something to use to knock it open, but the whole house was lit up in flame. Around him, wood sputtered and ceilings split and beams cracked with a sound like bones breaking. One lone tapestry still clung to the walls. Frederick pulled it from the wall before it caught flame, and batted away the fire on the floor next to the door. Using the tapestry to shield his hand, the urn under his shirt, Frederick placed the tapestry over the doorknob and turned. The door opened—he was out. Frederick dove out the door and onto the portico, rolling the small sparks of flame off his body in the grass. He leapt to his feet—running and coughing and sweating. His lungs and nose burned, still filled with the poisonous, scorching smoke. His one shoe was gone and the other had burned through in spots. It smelled awful, like charred hair. But Frederick didn't care. He ran through the glorious cool air of the night garden, not stopping for breath until he'd reached the fruit trees, where he knew that he was safe for a minute.

Doubled over from the run, Frederick stopped and reclaimed his breath. He was shivering now, and his teeth chattered loudly in his mouth. His bones felt hollow in his body, like twigs for the cinders. Blood coursed through him like a river of fire. His feet were torn up, and his skin was burnt, in some places too tender to touch.

But he'd made it out, and he had the map! The urn was still wrapped under his shirt.

Frederick collapsed to the ground, letting the cool blades brush against his face, coughing and coughing. The scent of anything other than smoke was a relief. Frederick inhaled the moist, grassy ground.

When he sat up, Frederick watched through the trees with horror as what was left of the President's House burned and burned. It went from a giant cloud of orange, tinged blue at the bottom, to a smoky gray that blew all around, some of the smoke reaching Frederick. He stayed where he was, hypnotized by the sight. He knew he wasn't yet safe, but he was too exhausted to move. It was all he could do to crawl into the bushes, where sleep claimed him.

Frederick awoke before dawn to the sound of the bushes rustling. He jumped to his charred feet. Thunder crashed above, and the air was thick and musty. Wind rattled the branches in the orchard, whistling through the leaves. Was there someone else in the garden?

Frederick hid behind a tree while his thoughts rushed forward. He was now in occupied Washington. The British had seized the city, and Frederick would have to get out without being seen. He picked up the urn with the map on it, safe beneath some leaves. The general would be in Baltimore by now, Frederick hoped, wishing he'd told him that the ring was in Canada. It would have put more space between them.

Frederick peeked around. Gardens, trees, bushes, statues.

And then — a flash of red. The V-shaped scar.

The gunshot rattled the bush just next to him but Frederick was already on the move.

He took off with the map through the orchards as fast as he could, his shoeless feet taking a beating with each step.

"You!" General V cried, gaining on Frederick as they ran through the grounds. "The map was a fake!"

Oh, no! Frederick didn't know how he would out-run the general. His lungs were still weak from the day before.

Thunder clapped, sending a rumble through the grounds. Lightning flashed through the sky in white-hot forks. Rain pattered down, and the splattering of trees and dirt made it hard to hear how close General V was behind him.

Frederick ran as fast as he could back through the orchards, rain soaking his clothes. He dashed out the gate and down the deserted Washington streets, the city a rubble of ashes, his feet slapping hard against the wet ground, the urn pressed in close to his belly. He turned back to see General V slip on a pile of slick leaves. *Lose him! Now!*

Tearing past the farms and acres from yesterday, Frederick fought his way back toward the Potomac. He spotted British troops out of the corner of his eye, and veered diagonally, still running toward the Mall.

The green was wide open, a straight shot, but there were more British troops lined all along the edges. Frederick didn't have a weapon; he had nothing except the urn.

He broke into the fastest sprint he'd ever run.

"Hey! Stop! You! You're not allowed here!" an officer called from horseback, chasing after him. Three more horses followed.

The soldier whistled, and more soldiers on horseback gathered to chase Frederick. The redcoats flooded onto the Mall — he was surrounded!

Frederick turned around. Was it too late to cross back? He threw a frantic look over his shoulder and saw, to his horror, the general only twenty paces away. There was no choice. Frederick plunged into the maze of soldiers and horses. A red-sleeved arm snaked out to catch him, but he ducked and spun, colliding with the flank of a rust-colored Arabian. It reared, throwing the officer from its back, and Frederick used the distraction to weave through the crush of bodies.

He had one chance to make it off the Mall—one chance that would either succeed beautifully or lead to his demise.

Running full speed, Frederick held the urn with one hand and leapt face-first for the wet grass. His arms slid along the green, gliding his body forward fast enough to rocket himself beneath the horses' legs in front of him. Mud spattered his face and neck. His chin bumped over the ground, but the grass was slick enough to push Frederick underneath the last row of horses and through to the other side.

I've made it! thought Frederick.

Through the sheets of rain falling, Frederick spotted a bridge and made a dash for it. The rain made everything gray, including the bridge and the rapids below. Everything blended together. And so Frederick did not realize until he was halfway over the water that the other side of the bridge had collapsed. He was at the edge before he had to pull back, flailing his arms, to avoid falling into the rushing water below.

Frederick did not want to look down—the bridge was so much higher than he remembered. He kicked a stone over the edge and watched as it plummeted for what seemed like hours before the water seized it.

The current was high and fast, hurtling branches and trees in whirlpools of rushing water. Clouds gathered and raced across the sky, darkening the day. Frederick barely knew how to swim.

A shot exploded behind him. Frederick whirled

around to find the general on horseback behind him on the bridge, closing in quickly. Frederick had only one move left to him.

Urn pressed close with both arms, Frederick took a deep breath and jumped.

The water rushed over his face, hurtling him over rocks, slamming him against the riverbed, and then, as soon as Frederick emerged above the river and into the downpour, attempting to swim with one hand, he was submerged again under water, gasping for air and trying uselessly to fight the current, to break out of the swirling eddies that threatened to keep him trapped under.

Frederick's arms were leaden, and he could barely lift his legs enough to kick himself up. But he was alive. The storm battered the river and everything in it. Every bone in Frederick's body seemed to be telling him to give up, that he wouldn't make it. He was so tired he could hardly breathe in coughing gasps of rain as he thrashed against the river. Water pinched his lungs, but his hand still clutched the urn. *Must get the map to Cahills, map to Cahills*, he repeated to himself between breaths.

Frederick swung his head up, his arms flailing in the water, and caught a glimpse of General V still up on the bridge. Then lightning struck again, startling the general's horse. She whinnied and reared back, thrashing her head, and when the thunder crashed, the general was tossed out of his saddle. He flew through the air, a wide red arc against the dark sky.

"Nooooooooo," the general cried, his voice howling above the wind as he hurtled toward the river.

His head cracked against a boulder that jutted up from the river and his body went limp, crashing like a cannonball into the water. The splash it sent up nearly reached the bridge.

He was dead.

But Frederick himself could barely stay afloat. He took one last big breath and kicked against the river, propelling himself roughly toward the bank. Frederick swam until the river grew more shallow, more tame. He reached a sloping bank and beached himself against a sapling, his heart beating rapidly and his clothes heavy on his soaking body.

Frederick stayed there, sheltered under the small tree, while the storm raged around him. Lightning and thunder boomed and boomed, until at last the claps grew less frequent and the storm quieted. The rain was still falling, but the sky was lighter now, the clouds blowing over.

Now there's only the entire British army to avoid.

Frederick pulled himself out of the water and trudged toward safety. Dolley had told him about a camp where her husband would join her when it was safe.

It was a long way off.

His clothes were cold, and the skin on his feet felt tender without his shoes. His elbow still ached from smashing the window, and even on solid ground, Frederick still felt as if the river were rushing beneath him.

Whenever he heard voices, Frederick jumped behind a tree. He did not want to risk crossing a British officer again. And he was certain he would scare regular citizens with the way he looked — he rivaled the soldiers coming home from war in his current condition.

He missed his parents.

He would have given anything to tell them what had happened in the last twenty-four hours.

It was as if he was pressing on through in a cold and rainy dream.

Frederick trundled past village after village on his way to the camp. He passed general stores and churches, taverns and schoolhouses, before the smell of campfire smoke reached out to him.

Something delicious was roasting over coals — fish, Frederick guessed, with the river right here. He followed his nose down the road.

Could this be it?

A sea of tents had been erected, and tarp after tarp was strung between trees. Frederick picked his way through camp toward the largest campfire, which was circled by a group of military men. There, in the middle of the laughter, he spotted Dolley.

Frederick rushed to see her.

"Oh, Frederick!" Dolley cried, running to greet him. "Gentlemen, this is the young man who saved my life!"

She enveloped him in a bear hug and Frederick couldn't remember the last time he had been so happy to see someone. She somehow managed to still look fresh and clean, even after a night spent at this muddied campsite.

As Frederick lowered his arms, Dolley bumped her hand against the urn. Frederick hadn't realized it was still gripped tightly in his hands.

She searched his face quizzically, but before he could answer, she put her finger to her lips. *Shhh.* Her face broke out into a grin as they moved out of earshot.

The men can't know, he thought.

"Mrs. Madison," he said, "I managed to pull a gift out of the President's House for you, just before I escaped."

"Why thank you, Frederick Warren," Dolley said, playing along. "Wherever did you find it?"

"Doesn't matter," he said lightly. "Flip it over."

Frederick watched as Dolley's eyes widened as large as saucers when she saw the map. She looked up at him, amazed. "But you—how did you—and the general?!"

"He won't be bothering us now."

Dolley shook her head and took his arm. "Come with me, Frederick. There are some people I want you to see."

She led him deeper into the encampment to a simple shelter in the woods, and nodded at an American soldier positioned under a tree. Inside the tent there were benches set up inside, and crates flipped over to sit on, as well as a few soft-looking cots that were calling out to Frederick.

Am I going to meet the president?

But it was Frederick's parents waiting for him instead, huddled close around a carved wooden table, their faces streaked with grief.

When they lifted their eyes to see him standing in the tent, their expressions gave way to a miraculous relief, and they scrambled to embrace him, squeezing him tight. His burns smarted at the contact, but then he leaned in to hug them harder.

"Oh, Frederick, we were so worried!" his mother exclaimed, clutching him close.

"Are you all right?"

His father clapped his back, another sore spot, and embraced him strongly, crying, "Son, son, Mrs. Madison wasn't sure you had escaped! We were afraid—" He didn't let himself finish the sentence. "What happened to you?"

"Frederick, your shoes! Your face, what happened to this elbow? You'll need stitches. . . ." Wilhelmina Warren cupped his muddy chin in her hand and met his eyes.

Slowly, Frederick eased into a rickety chair, one parent on each side. "I was afraid I'd never see you both again."

Frederick was shivering, so Dolley brought him some tea while Frederick described Ramsay's arrival. The liquid coated his throat in honeyed sweetness.

"Oh, Frederick, how awful," his mother murmured, rubbing a tear at his shoulder. "You must have been so frightened."

"I was terrified," Frederick said. "When I got to the President's House, the president was gone, but the first lady and I searched and searched, and she was able to get out before the fire."

"You were very brave," his father said. Frederick hadn't felt courageous when he'd been in the basement, or during the fire, or swimming through the river, but all of it rushed through him now. Frederick lifted his chest with pride.

Yes. Frederick nodded. *I was serious for once.*

"No one could expect you to swipe the map from under the Vespers' noses *while* the British were attacking," his father continued. "Not even the most experienced agents would be expected to pull off a feat like that. I can't tell you how proud your mother and I are."

Frederick's parents looked at him in awe and then at the urn Dolley brought out to show them. Dolley placed food in front of Frederick while his parents ran their fingers reverently over the Madrigal map.

Dolley smiled at Frederick and said, "When's our next mission, partner?"

Frederick grinned back at her. He knew his family would never be the same. Instead of two secret agents running the inn, now there were three.

Weeks later, when they set out to retrieve Gideon's ring, it was Frederick who led the way.

THE HOUDINI ESCAPE

PART 2

New York City, 1891

It was the final show of the night, and the eyes of every person crammed inside the tent were trained on him. Harry "the King of Cards" Weiss advanced down the aisle, his voice filling the cramped space as he told the story of the four kings. They were brothers whose mother had been forced to send them away at birth, which he illustrated by shuffling the four king cards into the deck.

As the audience bought into the story, Harry's voice grew steadier. He might be only a teenager, but he knew that he needed to speak with the confidence and poise of a veteran magician. Harry could feel the excitement build as he wove a tale of each brother going on his own path and becoming king of a distant land.

As he neared the stage, he brushed against a boy leaning in too close, and with an undetectable motion, Harry slipped the queen of hearts into the boy's pocket. There was a reason the light in the tent was kept dim.

Harry reached the stage, turned, and held out the deck in his left hand. "Now, these four kings were separated at birth. But one day, they all traveled back to their home for a reunion." He stared down at the deck and wrinkled his brow. The audience would expect him to pull the four cards out of the deck, but instead, Harry palmed the cards from a hidden pocket.

"The king of diamonds, the great merchant, came from the west," he said as the card appeared in his right hand. He knew that, to the audience, it would look like it had materialized out of thin air. "The king of hearts, the great poet, came from the east. The king of spades, the great architect, came from the north. And the king of clubs, the great warrior, came from the south."

The audience applauded, and Harry grinned. Breathing a sigh of relief, he felt like a king in his own right. Every magician used sleight of hand like palming cards, but Harry always worried that someone would catch him, or call him out. Now, the hard part was over. All that was left was the triumphant final reveal, the moment that made everything worth it: the countless hours practicing, the smell of sweat and smoke that filled the tent, the worried expression on his parents' faces whenever he talked about magic.

"But what about the poor mother, who was forced to send her sons to the four corners of the earth?" Harry could feel the anticipation growing. Surprising an audience was one thing. Getting them to go along with the story was what gave him a rush. "Yes, their mother, the queen of hearts—she was supposed to be there, too. But where was she?"

Harry looked around, miming a search. Finally, he peered out into the audience.

"I can't seem to find her. You, boy," he said, pointing at the child he'd identified earlier. "Do you know where the queen is?"

The boy shook his head mutely.

"Hm. Maybe you should check your pocket. You never know what might be in there."

The boy looked confused, but checked his pocket. Harry grinned. In a moment, the queen of hearts would meet her sons, the reunion would be complete, and Harry would bow out to a standing ovation.

The boy came up empty, and Harry chuckled. "Maybe your other pocket," he said with ease.

The boy stuck his hand into the other jacket pocket. As the bewildered audience member checked his pants, Harry's stomach tied itself in knots. What had gone wrong? He knew he had dropped the card in the boy's pocket.

"It's there somewhere, ain't it?" Harry demanded, his practiced performer voice falling away like a piece of cheap scenery.

The boy began to pat his jacket anxiously, and even searched the ground around his feet.

"I'm sorry," the boy said, looking up at him with wide eyes. "I don't have it."

The audience began to fidget, and the tent filled with the sound of whispers and a few snickers. Harry's mind raced, but when he opened his mouth to improvise an excuse, nothing came out. In an instant, the confident showman was gone. Suddenly, the King of Cards was just Harry, the immigrant kid with the funny accent who worked in a tie factory.

As soon as a few smirking teenagers stood to go, it was over. Within moments, the audience was shuffling out of the tent, muttering about wasting their money on some hack.

Even before the last audience member had left the tent, it hit him. He had gone for the wrong boy. Harry grimaced. Somehow he had gotten turned around. In the dim light, they all looked the same. It had been the boy on the other side of the aisle.

He wanted to run outside and yell, to call them back and demand that they see that the trick really had worked. But it was too late. Harry sighed and began shuffling around the stage to pack up. Other magicians had chests, trap doors, and trick mirrors, but he had to make do with the simplest tools: silk handkerchiefs that he could force to change colors, rings that he could separate and connect, and several decks of cards.

Harry froze as the distinct smell of cigar smoke

and cheap whiskey filled his nose. Out of the corner of his eye, he saw the tent flap open, and the portly ringmaster stormed inside. Harry faced the back wall and concentrated on refolding his silk handkerchiefs, unwilling to face the ringmaster, Thaddeus. The smell grew stronger and the low stage creaked as the heavy man stepped up.

"You better have a good explanation for what happened out there," he said, grabbing Harry by the collar. Harry suppressed a groan. The other seven shows he'd performed that day had gone perfectly. But of course Thaddeus had only seen the one he botched.

Harry turned around to face him. The man was standing close, his girth practically bursting the buttons on his bright red jacket. "I'm sorry, but—"

"Quiet," the ringmaster snapped before taking another puff of his cigar. "I billed you as the King of Cards. My show's about sparkle, pizzazz . . . ya know, *magic*. The king of something doesn't lose track of his card! Three of them had the nerve to ask for refunds! I didn't give 'em money, but I had Larson give them free hot sausages. All because you can't find the queen!"

Harry felt his heart speed up. "It won't happen again. I promise." If he lost this job, it could take months to find another magician gig. He'd probably have to take extra shifts at the factory. His family counted on the income from his weekend job—he couldn't come home empty-handed.

Thaddeus glared at him. "You made the show look

bad, kid. People will talk. I'll lose ticket sales from this, no doubt about it."

Harry's shoulders tensed as he imagined the look on his parents' faces when he told them he lost the job. His mother had been endlessly patient when he first started practicing, letting him find her card over and over again, never letting on when she realized his method. His father, on the other hand, had always tried to uncover the secret, which had taught Harry one of the most important rules of magic: never perform the same trick twice in a row. But now it looked like all his hard work would go to waste.

The ringmaster twirled his mustache and sighed. "I can't pay a magician who doesn't do magic. One more mistake and you're done. And I'll spread the word to the rest of the town." He started lumbering toward the front of the tent, but then turned to look over his shoulder. "Unless you double your ticket sales next weekend, you'll never work Coney Island again."

The flap closed, leaving Harry alone with nothing but his flimsy props and empty pockets. He had just enough for the horsecar fare, but nothing to give his mother for the grocer. Weighed down by a heaviness that started in his stomach and extended to his feet, Harry blew out the lamps in the tent and headed out into the Coney Island night.

Harry trudged along the deserted boardwalk on his way to the horsecar that would take him from Coney Island back to Manhattan. The families were all gone and the lights were off, taking with them any sense of festivity. Now it was just carnies tearing down their tents or trying to entice the loitering teenagers to take one last ride on the Switchback Railway.

He saw one older man playing Bottle Up, attempting to use a ring on a string to put a bottle upright. Harry shook his head when he noticed the smudge of chalk on the back of the man's shabby jacket. That meant he was "marked," a fool who had lost a pile of money at one game — and could likely be suckered into losing more at another booth. The bright lights of Coney Island were the first thing many immigrants saw in New York — the ships passed the boardwalk even before the Statue of Liberty — and the new arrivals would often come soon after leaving Ellis Island, much to the delight of the con men, who knew how to take advantage of them.

Harry sped up to pass several grim-looking men huddled in an alleyway, exchanging money. He glanced in the opposite direction, pretending to be interested in the barking dogs outside the racetrack. The men were probably selling stolen goods, but it was none of his concern. And everyone knew that Police Chief McKane looked the other way. That is, if he and his captains weren't actually in on the deal.

Harry worked for Thaddeus, so no one bothered

him. But that hadn't always been true. The first time he'd tried to perform magic on the street, three burly men had tried to "teach him a lesson" about respecting other people's "territory." Luckily, Harry was a track champion at the Pastime Athletic Club, and he easily outdistanced them, but he ran into similar problems until Thaddeus saw him doing his act at a dime museum in Queens and hired him to perform weekends in his show.

Even after tonight's disappointment, Harry was still proud to be performing in Coney Island. He might be between the bearded ladies (women with glue and hair) and the unicorn (an unfortunate horse, glue, and the horn of an even more unfortunate narwhal), but he was a showman with a real show.

His father sometimes talked about the great performers and artists that he was related to as members of the Cahill Family. He even claimed that creative geniuses like Mozart and Lord Byron were among their distant cousins, though it was hard to imagine his serious father, a former rabbi, having anything to do with such colorful figures. Harry longed to take the stage like his ancestors had—but his parents had made it clear that his main obligation was to help support the family.

Harry wanted to be useful. He knew how much his parents worried about money, especially now that his father was too ill to work. But he wished they believed he could do better as a performer than he could cutting ties. Harry knew lifers at the factory, grizzled men and women who had been doing the same job for decades and making the same pay. They didn't starve, but they never got ahead, either. They just sat at the same work-table day after day, slowly withering away.

The wait for the horsecar, a horse-drawn wagon that carried about fifteen people, was brief. Normally he would have been happy to be home sooner, but even with work in the morning, Harry wasn't eager to face his family. He hung back at the end of the line before reluctantly giving the driver his last pennies and crowding onto the carriage with the carnival tourists and workers returning to Manhattan.

The horsecar bumped its way through Brooklyn. It was starting to get late, but the streets were still crowded. Omnibuses full of men in hats wove between endless rows of wooden stands where vendors made their final sales pitches, hoping to sell their remaining wares at discount prices before heading home. Grubby children played in the street, dashing between the horses and skirting around the ash barrels that stood overflowing on every corner.

He changed horsecars, and slumped in the back as the coach bumped over the Brooklyn Bridge. Although the sky was dark, the electric lights in the new build-ings allowed Harry to make out the silhouette of the skyline—the skeleton frames of the new skyscrapers looming over the smaller structures.

Next to him, a group of Chinese workers played a

betting game that involved guessing the number of beads in a bowl. Each time someone won, the whole group would erupt in cheers. Harry watched out of the corner of his eye. With his sleight of hand, he knew he could make money at a game like that, but he'd seen what happened to cheaters who were caught in Coney Island. Sleight of hand got a lot harder if your hand was missing a few fingers.

As they traveled uptown, the streetlights grew farther apart and the city settled into sleep. After another horsecar change and a walk of several blocks, Harry arrived at West 113th Street, where he lived with his parents and five siblings. His stomach rumbled as he walked up the stairs to his family's town house. He hoped there were leftovers from dinner for him to eat. Without the money from his show, there was no knowing what tomorrow would bring.

The house was dark, and Harry let himself in as quietly as he could. He'd forgotten his key again, but that was no problem — a few seconds with the pick from his bag of magicians' tools and the lock was open. Ever since his brief apprenticeship to a locksmith back in Appleton, Wisconsin, Harry had been trying to think of ways to incorporate his skills into his act, but kept coming up short. He couldn't imagine anything less exciting than someone picking a lock onstage.

He padded through the hallway, anxious to make sure he didn't wake his family. But as he crossed the darkened parlor, he stepped on something that crunched like broken glass. Harry shook his head. One of his siblings must have broken something again. He reached toward the sideboard and fumbled for a moment before his hands found the gas lamp and matches.

As the light filled the room with long shadows and a dim orange glow, Harry's breath caught in his chest. His family's keepsakes, which normally stood proudly on the mantel, were all smashed. Portraits, his father's awards, Harry's cross-country medals, and even the crystal glasses from his parents' wedding had been reduced to a pile of fragments and shards. It had not been done recklessly — the only way to cause this type of damage was to crush each piece individually. A terrifying thought planted itself in his mind, and coils of dread tightened around his stomach. What if someone had hurt his family?

He raised the lamp, revealing deep scratches in the wall above the mantel, slashes that looked like the letter V. Harry stepped back and slipped on a piece of the wreckage, too shocked to even try to find his balance. He sent a chair flying as he fell, and landed with a thump, still clutching the gas lamp.

As Harry pulled himself to his feet, he could hear his parents stirring in their room. The door opened and his mother appeared. Harry darted forward to stop her from entering, but it was too late. She gasped as she took in the scene, turning around to clutch Harry's father as he cautiously shuffled into the room.

"I thought you said they wouldn't bother us here," she whispered. "They came into our home." She brought her hand to her chest. "While we were *sleeping*."

His father's face was unreadable as he surveyed the scene. "Harry, go to bed." Since he'd fallen ill, Mayer Samuel's voice had grown thin, a crushing blow to the former rabbi who'd once transfixed crowded synagogues with his authoritative baritone. "Your mother and I will take care of this."

"What h-h-appened? Who . . . ?" Harry stammered.

When his mother saw the concern on Harry's face, she forced her mouth into a weak impression of a smile. "Don't worry. It looks like someone must have broken in. But they're gone now. We'll report it to the police in the morning."

Harry knew she was lying or at least hiding the truth. He raised an eyebrow at his father, hoping for a better explanation.

"Mother?" a girl's voice squeaked from the doorway. Harry's sister Carrie and brother Leopold were standing there in their nightshirts.

"It's nothing, dear," his mother said, shepherding them through the door and back to their room.

"What's really going on?" Harry asked his father once they were gone.

His father said nothing and shook his head, lowering himself wearily into his favorite chair.

Unwilling to leave, Harry bent down and started cleaning up. He salvaged the few pieces that still had some value, and swept the rest of the wreckage into a pile.

"Thank you, Harry," his father said, and then fell silent again as Harry swept the debris into a dustpan and emptied it into an old sack.

"How were your shows?" Mayer Samuel finally asked, as if changing the subject could hide the fact that something terrible had happened. Harry felt a flash of irritation. If he was old enough to support his family, then he was old enough to know the truth about the break-in. But before he had the chance to release the cutting words forming in his throat, Harry caught a glance of his father's weary face and softened. "Not great," he admitted. "I bungled the last trick, and Thaddeus refused to pay me." When his father didn't respond, Harry continued. "If I make another mistake, I'm out forever," he said flatly, feeling his last tendril of hope shriveling as he admitted it.

His father just looked at the floor. Harry knew he was disappointed, but too kind to say anything while the wound was still fresh.

"Harry, why do you keep doing this to yourself?" his mother asked from the doorway. "You'll drive yourself mad trying to make a living from magic. Don't you want a steady income? Or the ability to support a family?"

Harry clenched and unclenched his fists.

"Someone breaks into our house, shatters our valuables, and carves our wall . . . and you want to talk about my job prospects?" he retorted.

"Your mother and I will handle it," his father said quietly. "An old acquaintance just wanted to send me . . . a message. I'll make him see reason and we'll work something out."

"We want what's best for you, and for the family," his mother added. "I know performing is your dream, but it's time for you to start thinking about your future."

Grateful that his parents couldn't see his flushing cheeks in the half light, Harry mumbled a hurried good night and headed to the room he shared with his brother Theo. His mother was right. As much as he hated it, he needed to take responsibility. He wouldn't go back to Coney Island next weekend. Instead he would ask the foreman if he could take extra shifts at the necktie factory.

As he tossed and turned in bed, he could hear his parents whispering in the parlor, their voices wavering between anger and fear. Harry strained to listen, but he couldn't make out their words until nearly an hour later, when his father spoke while passing his room: "It's my debt, Cecilia. I have to pay it one way or another."

Harry's scissors snipped, and the shape of a tie emerged from the striped cloth. He laid it carefully on the cart and grabbed another sheet of fabric, deftly maneuvering the blade until another tie appeared. Harry placed it on the cart, and waved one of the younger boys over to deliver the pile to the sewing table.

The air in R. H. Richter's tie factory was a symphony of production. Scissors snapped, carts squeaked, and from the other room came the lilt of the seamstresses' gossiping. He had liked it better when he was younger, pushing carts from room to room to keep the production flowing. He'd even carried a pack of cards with him to entertain the younger cutters when he had a free moment and the foreman wasn't around to yell at him.

But the idea of spending the rest of his life here filled Harry's stomach with dread. Day in, day out, he cut the same shape out of fabric. Every few weeks, the color or pattern of the material would change. Today, it was black and gold stripes. But there were no new challenges, no opportunities to use his imagination, or even his *brain*. The sun gleaming through the dirty windows seemed to creep across the sky more slowly each hour. And whenever he looked at the older men and women who had spent their lives in the factory, he could almost see himself in their weathered skin and resigned expressions.

It was a small mercy, but at least he had his friend Jacob next to him, scissors snipping out a monotonous counterpoint to Harry's own. "I've got your book,"

Jacob whispered when the foreman turned his back to them. After saving up for weeks, Harry had finally been able to buy a secondhand copy of a book written by the greatest magician of the modern world, Jean-Eugène Robert-Houdin. Harry had stayed up all night reading about Robert-Houdin's accomplishments: He read minds, brought orange trees to life, and even suspended his son in midair. Before Robert-Houdin, magicians had been limited to performing at fairs and on street corners, but he had raised magic to an art. He had owned his own theaters, performed for kings and queens, and had even been sent to Algeria by Napoleon III to use his magic to discredit a gang of con men gaining influence with faux-magical abilities.

The book had opened Harry to the world of possibility, to the chance that magic could be his ticket out of the soul-crushing tedium of factory life. But that had been nothing more than a child's foolish dream. "You can keep it."

"What are you talking about? It's your prized possession."

"I'm not doing magic anymore," Harry said flatly. "I need to focus on helping my family."

"You *can't*," Jacob exclaimed, then glanced around, relieved to see that the foreman wasn't looking their way. "Not after all the work we've put in. And besides, I've seen what happens when you perform. You become a completely different person, Harry. It's what you were meant to do!"

The two had been practicing magic in their spare time for a year now, performing together at various sideshows. When Harry's father had become too ill to work, a spot in the factory had opened up, and Harry had convinced the foreman to hire Jacob as a cutter.

Harry turned away. "I'm just not good enough at magic to support my family." He finished a tie and carefully laid it on the cart.

"How many times have you told me how you want to be just like Robert-Houdin?"

"We'll never get the money to build illusions like he had," Harry said, struggling to keep his voice low. "He used magnets and clockwork and had a crew of assistants, a carpenter, and a mechanic. He could make an orange tree blossom!"

"But what about the metamorphosis trick we talked about?" Jacob asked. "It requires a special prop, but we could afford it if we saved up."

"You don't get it," Harry snapped. "I'm done. I have to help my parents provide for my family. I can't spend money on magic boxes."

The foreman's heels clicked at the end of the hallway and the boys returned to their work. Harry's hands had learned the motions long ago and could cut out a necktie almost automatically.

Maybe one day, if he got a promotion and his father got better and came back to work, he would be able to afford to build a great trick. The thought of performing the metamorphosis filled him with new energy as he imagined the look on the audience's faces as they realized that he and Jacob had "magically" switched places while one of them was locked in a box.

Harry's mind raced as he thought about how the trick would work. Were there ways to make the switch faster? There were definitely ways to improve on the design of the box. If only he could talk it over with a carpenter . . .

A hand clamped on Harry's shoulder, and as he snapped back to reality his scissors slipped, cutting too far into the fabric. "What are you doing?" Harry yelped, before turning to see who it was. "You ruined this tie!"

The massive foreman loomed over him ominously. He looked like he belonged in a construction crew, or at the head of a Roman legion, instead of working in a tie factory. But Harry knew that he had been wounded during the Civil War, and hadn't been able to move easily in over two decades.

"You ruined it before I got here, Weiss," the foreman rumbled.

Harry glanced down. Sure enough, he had cut straight across the fabric rather than at an angle, leaving the tie with the stripes going straight across. He gulped. The whole batch was unsellable.

"I'm sorry," Harry said meekly. "My mind must have wandered."

"Weiss," the foreman growled. "Look at your cart."

Harry looked over at the cart. His heart sank. Every

single one of the ties was cut at the wrong angle. The room filled with a busy silence as the other workers stared intently at their task, pretending not to listen.

"You immigrants are all the same," the foreman said, his lips curling with disgust. "You always want a job, but you never want to work. You know the rule: You don't pay attention, you don't get paid." He shook his head and pointed to the door. "Get out of here. And don't bother coming back."

Jacob looked up for a split second, catching Harry's eye with a panicked look. Then he turned and bent back to his cutting. They knew from experience how quickly the foreman's anger could shift focus.

"But my family—" Harry protested.

"I said get *out*," the foreman spat. "You're lucky I'm not making you pay for all this wasted cloth. You better leave before I change my mind."

Harry stood up in a daze, and took a step before realizing that he was still holding his scissors. The foreman held out his hand and Harry automatically handed them over. He walked out into the sunlit street, still bewildered by what had just taken place. In less than twenty-four hours, he'd managed to lose two jobs. He wasn't cut out to be a magician, and apparently, he didn't even have what it took to work in a factory.

"Watch it." Harry stepped to the side as a woman holding a large basket brushed past him, shooting him a nasty look. The street was packed with people rushing in all directions, but Harry simply stood and stared. Normally, the crowds and the noise filled Harry with a sense of excitement, but today, they just made him feel terribly alone.

Shops and pedestrians flashed by as Harry jogged up Broadway. He didn't have money for a horsecar, and running was the only way to loosen the knot of guilt and fear that had started growing in his stomach as he left the tie factory.

He'd spent the first few hours wandering around the garment district. Racks of clothes lined the streets, made by immigrants like Harry, and sold to the middle-class women who could afford new clothes for their families. The salesmen stood outside, each trying to drown out the others with their promises about sup-plying the latest fashions for the lowest price. There were black and gray waistcoats for the men, and long ladies' dresses edged with ruffles and frills. For the more daring, there were special ladies' costumes for bicycling, complete with pants.

He'd looked to see if any of the stores were hiring, but every one seemed full up. Finally, he'd decided that there was nothing left to do but to head home and tell his family what had happened. He walked the first few miles until the factories and shops gave way to crowded apartment buildings and crumbling houses, and then he began to run. He'd learned the hard way what happened to immigrant boys who dashed through the fancy residential areas—once he'd been stopped by a policeman who thought that Harry was a thief escaping from the scene of a crime.

With a few detours, it was a perfect five-mile course from the garment district to his family's home on 113th Street in Harlem. His dedication had made him a champion runner at the Pastime Athletic Club, and he had even won a medal last year in a citywide competition. When he'd been asked to pose for the local paper after his win in the cross-country meet, he'd bought a handful of medals from a trinket shop on Coney Island and stuck them across his uniform. The reporter had seemed skeptical, but the photographer ate it up. Being a stage performer had taught Harry that making an impression mattered. And it wasn't like Harry had actually said that he won the medals. People saw what they wanted to see—it wasn't his fault if they made assumptions that weren't true.

As Harry turned the corner onto his block, he saw three men knocking on the door of his family's town house. By the time he ran up the steps, they had already been let inside and Harry could hear them talking with his father. He entered quietly and stopped a moment in the foyer, allowing his eyes to settle on the wooden staircase that had once been finely crafted, but was now chipped and worn. As Harry paused a moment, reluctant to go up and face his parents, his father's voice filtered down the stairs.

"You must understand, I've been trying," his father was saying. "I've fallen a bit ill. But I am resting, and I have faith that it will pass."

The man at the other end of the conversation said something softly. It sounded like he had a Hungarian accent, but Harry couldn't make out the words. He knew he shouldn't eavesdrop, but he couldn't force himself to go up the stairs or back out the door.

"I just don't have the money," his father continued. "We're close to losing the house as it is. . . ." His father's voice faltered.

Harry felt like he'd been punched in the gut for the second time in one day. His father owed these men money. Harry knew how these debts were accounted for in Coney Island—you either paid up, or someone would have to fish your body out of the harbor.

And this, of all days, was the day that he had lost his job.

"I have paid on time for years. Just give me a few extra weeks, and you'll have your money." Harry could hear the pleading in his father's voice.

There was silence from above. Harry hoped that it was the men reconsidering their position, but his hopes were dashed as he heard the Hungarian-accented voice speak in low, threatening tones.

"I understand," Mayer Samuel answered, his voice thin and reedy.

Harry heard the floorboards squeak as the men walked toward the stairs. After they'd left, Harry opened the door, slipped out, and began hurrying down the street.

When he was a few paces behind the men, he slowed to a walk, taking care to stay to the side in case they turned and he needed to duck into an alley. All three men wore expensive suits, but the one leading the way was carrying a silver walking stick, and his black hair was slicked back with oil. He had the erect posture that Harry associated with the elegant ringmasters who performed in the big circus tents at Coney Island. They made his own boss, ringmaster Thaddeus, look like a small-time crook. Which wasn't far from the truth. The man wrinkled his nose and walked more quickly as they passed two grubby boys playing in the gutter.

The men swaggered down the street, not bothering to look around, and Harry found himself following them. He had only intended to get a quick look, but as Harry replayed his father's words in his head, he grew desperate to find out who these people were. His father was a man of principle—how had he gotten mixed up with men who would break into his house and destroy his family's valuables?

The sun was setting, and Harry was easily able to trail them without raising suspicions. When they hailed a passing hansom cab, Harry jogged behind the plodding horse, keeping a safe distance and trying to stay in the shadows.

The cab wound through the edges of the city as the moon rose, passing factories that had emptied for the day, and a few that had electric lights installed. Finally, they turned down to the docks. For a moment, he thought he had fallen too far behind and lost them, but he turned a corner and saw the three men disembarking and the cab heading back into the city.

Harry slunk through the shadows as the men walked closer to the water, toward the smell of fish, coal, and garbage. The wooden piers that stretched out into the river were so long that they seemed to disappear into the night.

They had been met by a larger group of what looked to Harry like six policemen. For a hopeful moment Harry thought that the men were about to be arrested. If they were in jail, surely his family's debt wouldn't matter. But the two groups were simply talking, and Harry's heart sank as he saw the distinctive man with a bow tie, handlebar mustache, and beard who seemed to be in charge.

It was Police Chief McKane, the corrupt and despotic man who was behind every shady deal on Coney Island. He was also the fire commissioner, schools commissioner, public lands commissioner, superintendent of the Methodist Church, and head tenor in the church choir. He even played Santa Claus in the yearly Christmas pageant. Nothing went down in Coney Island without McKane's approval. He had been on trial multiple times, but the state authorities could never get the charges to stick.

McKane was speaking to the man with the slicked-back hair, whose name was apparently Zoltan. They were discussing a business deal that had evidently gone sour, for McKane was shouting, and his face had grown red. Occasionally, Zoltan would interject a few low words, but mostly he remained impassive, watching the police chief with an amused smile. Tension mounted between the observers, and finally, McKane reached for his gun.

Harry held his breath as the scene turned into a flurry of activity. Zoltan lunged for McKane, while his companions flew at the other policemen. For a moment, the sound of footsteps, shouts, and cracking bones echoed through the night air, but they soon gave way to a faint chorus of groans and labored breathing.

Zoltan had the police chief in a headlock and was holding a gleaming blade to his throat. His companions were standing over the pile of injured policemen on the ground. Harry gasped and took a few steps back into a shadowy alley. When he peered out again, he saw McKane involved in a very different sort of negotiation — one that had him pleading for his life.

Harry pressed his back against the wall and tried to make himself as small as possible. Following men like this was suicidal. They were obviously trained killers, and if they could take out a band of policemen, there was no knowing what they'd do to an unarmed kid.

Zoltan smiled and said something Harry couldn't hear. The terrified-looking police chief dug an item out of his pocket, shoved it into Zoltan's hands, and ran off into the night.

A few moments later, Harry heard the footsteps of the three men coming toward the alley. He ducked down as low as he could, trying to hold his breath despite the rank odor of the trash he was using as cover. Their pace slackened as they passed him, and Harry's heart felt like it slowed as well. Finally, the footsteps receded, and Harry waited a minute before he stood up.

He gingerly stepped over the trash, trying to avoid getting dirtier than he already was, then stretched his legs, which had fallen asleep from the combination of running and crouching.

Harry felt a brush of air, and before he could react an arm was wrapped around his chest and a knife was at his throat. A voice whispered in his ear, gravelly and threatening. "Who are you, boy?" He couldn't turn his head to see the man behind him, but he could smell the pungent oil in his hair. Down the street, he could see the other two men returning.

"I'm Harry," he blurted, catching himself before he gave away his last name.

"Why were you watching us?"

"I didn't—I wasn't—" Harry stuttered. The cold blade of the knife dug into his skin, and he could feel a drop of blood making a trail down his neck. "I was just sleeping there," he lied. "I got kicked out of my house."

"You chose a bad spot for a nap," the man growled

in his ear. He drew away and shoved Harry into the arms of the other two men. "Come."

His two companions grabbed Harry and dragged him forward. Harry tried to pull away, but they just gripped his arms tighter.

Harry's legs were shaking as he looked back and saw one of the policemen lying on the ground, moaning in pain. He should never have followed these men. It had been foolish to think that he could do anything to help his family. All he'd done was make things infinitely worse. And now, it looked like he might have to pay for his mistake with his life.

They led him onto the piers toward one of the boats, and dragged him up the gangway. "Where are we going?" Harry shouted, struggling against their grip. His legs skidded on the wood, unable to keep him balanced as the men hauled him forward. Were they going to take him with them? Lock him in the hold? *Torture* him?

They dragged Harry onto the deck of a small steamship, and a few minutes later, were pulling away from the pier, out onto the Hudson River.

Zoltan stepped forward and leaned in, so close that Harry could see his own reflection in the man's gray eyes. "I know who you are," he said coolly. His Hungarian accent was noticeable, but didn't sound like the other immigrants in Harry's neighborhood. His voice was more polished, as if he were used to speaking to—or maybe commanding—large groups of people. "You're Weiss's son. Did he send you to follow us?" Zoltan shook his head. "I expected him to know better."

"He didn't send me," Harry answered. "Please don't hurt him. I'll help pay back his debt. I work at a factory, and I'm taking extra shifts—"

Zoltan's face twitched, and Harry fell silent.

"Too late now," Zoltan said. "You weren't supposed to see any of that."

Harry could feel wind blowing across the deck as the steamship pulled out into the harbor. How long would it be before his parents started to worry? A surge of guilt briefly overwhelmed his fear. He didn't want to die, but the thought of his parents grieving him was almost worse.

Zoltan turned to address one of the other men. "Istvan, I know I've performed strangulation, suffocation, and premature burial, but have I done drowning?" Istvan shook his head. "Really? I can't believe I have such a hole in my repertoire." He shot Harry a smile that might have been considered winning had he not been discussing different methods of committing murder. "I have a reputation for a certain level of showmanship."

Harry felt his heart start to race. They weren't just trying to scare him. They were really going to do it. He winced as Istvan wrenched his arms behind his back while the third man went to the cabin and pulled out coils of rope.

"Are you sure we don't want to try my new Winchester rifle?" Istvan asked. "Or perhaps the wakizashi sword I bought off that Japanese merchant?"

Zoltan grinned. "Don't worry, I'm sure we'll find a way to employ your new toys soon."

Harry's stomach twisted, as if someone had already plunged a sword inside him. He imagined his mother's breakdown as she heard the news. His father's quiet resignation as the truth sank in and one more thread of his old life unraveled. His siblings would be crushed, but worse, who would even make the money to feed them? And Harry would never take the stage again. Never know the thrill of a perfectly executed illusion, and the cheers of a crowd enjoying being taken in.

He couldn't let this happen. He had to find a way to escape.

For a moment, Harry considered trying to fight them, but he knew that was pointless. There were three of them and they were all larger than he was. And there was probably more of a crew on the bridge and below deck. Harry breathed in and stood up straighter, almost as if he were onstage. A sense of calm and purpose settled over him. He couldn't overpower them, so he would have to survive some other way.

Feeling almost in a dream, he stepped forward and let them tie him up. As they looped the rope around his arms, he clenched his biceps. Harry had spent years performing as "Prince of the Air," and there was nothing for building muscle like hanging by your arms.

He flexed his muscles as they tightened the ropes and waited for them to move on to his feet before he relaxed them. Once his biceps were no longer clenched, he could feel that the ropes were significantly looser.

The fear and panic coursing through his body gave way to the same anxious energy he felt just before going onstage. But he couldn't let the men know he had a plan, and he allowed his body to go limp as Istvan carried him toward the rail. Harry's heart was pounding as he tried to squirm around to look out over the water. They were far from shore, but the lights of Manhattan were still visible.

"You don't need to do this," he yelled as they neared the rail. "My father will pay. I'll pay, too!" He needed to sound like he thought he was about to die. It wasn't difficult. Harry knew there was a high chance his plan would fail. But he couldn't dwell on that now.

It was showtime.

Istvan grunted and set him on the deck next to the rail. Harry looked down and grew slightly dizzy as he watched the choppy water splashing against the bottom of the ship about four stories below. "You don't have to do this!" Harry yelled, feeling a new wave of terror threatening to take over his body. "Please!"

Zoltan gave Harry a push. He teetered for a moment, staring at the dark water below. Then the boat lurched and he lost his balance and plunged overboard.

Harry took in a deep breath before he hit the surface and the icy water closed around him. He wiggled like a dolphin, swimming farther underwater. He needed time to escape before he came up for air.

He writhed and thrashed, using the looseness of the ropes around his arms to his best advantage. The chill of the water clamped down on him and he could hear nothing but a dull roar and the thudding of his own heart. The ropes were cutting at his skin but he barely noticed as he strained to extricate himself.

For a moment, his right wrist seemed trapped in a knotted loop, but with a painful wrench he pulled it out. His hands were free. With his legs still tied, Harry looked up. The lights from the ship filtered through the dark water, and he could just make out the outline of the steamship's hull.

His lungs were screaming for air, but with a stroke of his arms, Harry dove deeper into the water. He waved his bound legs like a fin. As he reached the ship's hull, he grabbed on to the barnacles underneath and hauled himself down. If he surfaced too soon, the Vespers would know he'd survived.

As he passed the keel, the ship's paddle swung into motion. Harry felt a moment of panic as it started to drag him backward. With a kick of his legs and rapid pulling of his arms, he moved away. His lungs were burning and he felt his head pounding as he strained for the surface.

Finally, he broke the water and gasped. Air

flooded into his lungs. In his ears, his ragged breathing sounded incredibly loud, but luckily the noise of the steam engine and paddles seemed to be drowning it out.

He could hear Zoltan and his companions talking on the other side of the boat, and as his air returned, he smiled with satisfaction.

Harry clung to the hull of the ship as it began to gain speed and pull out of the harbor. Holding on with one hand, he used the other to untie his feet. The wet ropes seemed to stick to each other, but he finally got them untangled and let them sink into the water.

"He's not coming back up," Harry heard Istvan's voice carrying from the other side of the ship. "Looks like he's too small and skinny to float. I win. You owe me ten dollars, Bjorn."

"The ship started moving. We weren't close enough to see," Bjorn protested. "If I toss some dynamite in and blast-fish him out, would that count?"

"Enough," Zoltan cut in sharply. "We didn't come to America just to dispose of nosy children. It's time to get to work." He paused. "We'll finish this conversation below deck."

Even though he was clinging to the boat, Harry continued to tread water. In the freezing water, it was important to keep moving to stave off hypothermia.

As the steamship moved past Governor's Island, they passed a garbage scow headed back toward the city. Harry pushed off and set out with vigorous strokes. He latched on to the scow as it chugged past and hauled himself on board. The captain of the tugboat might see him, but Harry hardly cared. He was out of the freezing water, and would be back in the city within minutes.

And if he'd planned correctly, Zoltan and his crew would think he was dead—which meant he was safe, for now. As he stripped off his soaked clothing and huddled down, Harry watched the steamship glide out into the bay until it disappeared into the night, leaving only the trails of its smokestacks.

"What were you thinking?" Harry's father demanded. "You were very nearly killed! Zoltan is a murderer. The Vespers use him for their most dangerous missions—they only sent him to collect my debt because he was in New York on other business."

It had been late when Harry returned, but his parents had been waiting for him. Early dawn light was coming through the parlor windows, and Harry could hear the city around them starting to wake up. His father's face was white from his illness, and he had an extra blanket draped over his legs.

"Who are the Vespers?" Harry asked, too tired from the events of the night to try to defend himself. "What do they want with our family?"

Harry's father sighed, and paused for a moment.

Finally, he looked up, fixing Harry with a sad stare. "You're too young to remember this, but life wasn't easy in Hungary, especially for Jews. I spent many years trying to arrange for us to come to America, but when the paperwork finally came through, we still didn't have enough money for the passage. I took a loan from the Vespers in order to buy a ticket for myself, and to leave behind enough money for you, your mother, and your four brothers to come over."

His father turned to his mother, who nodded silently, urging Mayer Samuel to continue. "It was foolish," he admitted. "At the time, I didn't know much about the Vespers. I understood that they had some sort of vendetta against the Cahills, but they were the only people in Budapest willing to lend that kind of money without any sort of collateral." He closed his eyes, as if recalling memories stored deep within his mind. "And now I know why. The Vespers are a worldwide network of criminals, and I should have never gotten involved with them."

"Why didn't you pay them back?" Harry asked.

His father shook his head. "I did. I tried. But they kept raising the interest until the payments became impossible." He gestured toward their sparsely furnished living room. "We've given them all we have."

"That's why we've been so demanding with you and your brothers," his mother added sadly. "We had no choice but to save up to try to pay them. We knew they would find us eventually."

Harry couldn't believe what he was hearing. "So they were the ones who broke into our house?" His father nodded. "We have to do something," Harry insisted. "I'll go to the police."

"You will do no such thing," Mayer Samuel commanded, his voice regaining some of its old authority. "The Vespers control every major crime ring in the city. There's no knowing what sort of influence they have with the police. You'll only make things worse."

A surge of hot rage welled up from somewhere deep inside him. "Well, I have to do something. I'm not going to stand by while they threaten our family."

"Harry," his father said, fixing his son with a stare that made it clear he'd heard what happened at the tie factory. "All you need to focus on is finding employment. Go do your shows this weekend to bring in a little money, and then find a real job next week. I'm sorry. I wish things were different."

"What will happen to you?" Harry demanded. "Won't the Vespers come back?"

"I'll take care of it," Mayer Samuel said. "We'll scrape together as much money as we can before they come back next week. But the most important thing is that you stay out of sight. The Vespers can't know that you survived. Not after what you saw down by the docks."

"Father, what if I —"

"No." His father's voice became stronger for a moment, almost as if he were his old self. "I may not be around much longer. This was my mistake, and you have to let me handle it." Harry could see the thinness in his father's pale cheeks in a new light. Mayer Samuel was wasting away, and the man who used to pick up Harry and spin him around, letting him pretend to be an acrobat, was never coming back.

"Harry." His mother couldn't quite look him in the eye. "Please do as he says. You can't come back home until the Vespers return to Europe. Zoltan hates to be crossed, and he hates to make a mistake. If they see you, they will kill you . . . and then punish the rest of our family as well. Do you understand?"

Harry gulped. "I won't let them find me. I'll stay with Jacob until they leave. And once they're gone . . . I'll do my part to take care of the family. I swear it."

Harry offered the deck, and the girl pulled the top card off as instructed. The audience watched intently.

"It's the five of hearts. That was my card," she announced. "But what happened to . . ."

"I suppose it was on top of the deck all along," Harry joked. "Perhaps you simply imagined putting it in your pocket."

His brush with death had left him jittery, and up until the moment he stepped onstage his hands had been shaking. But by the time he started his first trick in each show, the usual calm settled over him. In the low light of the stage, he morphed into the King of Cards.

She checked her pocket. "It's gone!" she squealed. The audience cheered. Harry bowed, made a few cards appear and disappear, and stepped into the tiny back-stage to a final round of applause. He sat down heavily on the small wooden stool. The "backstage" was little more than a heavy piece of black fabric blocking an area of a few square feet from view. There was nothing back here but the chair, a few rags, a flask of water, and an old drum. He sat back and mopped his brow with a handkerchief. It was his fifteenth show that Saturday, and there was time left for another two. It took about ten minutes for the old crowd to leave and the new one to assemble. Every audience had a different feel, and Harry would often change the order of his tricks to keep the crowd engaged.

Harry had snuck out to Coney Island early that morning, desperately hoping to escape notice. New York was an enormous city and the chance of him run-ning into Zoltan or one of the other Vespers was tiny, but Harry's heart still leaped every time he saw a man with black hair.

He could hear Thaddeus outside his tent, urging fairgoers to see the amazing magician inside. From the way he spoke, it sounded like "the King of Cards" was capable of truly incredible feats. Harry just hoped that he was capable of the incredible feat of getting paid for his day's work.

Although it was a grueling life, realizing that this

was his last weekend of shows reminded Harry how much Coney Island felt like home. There were the circuses with high-flying acrobats and majestic lions. The ringmasters would bark out commands, drawing hundreds of eyes to every new spectacle. There were magicians who had devices that let them saw their assistants in half and make them disappear.

Harry knew how it was all done, of course, but he still let himself go along for the ride, clapping and hooting with the rest of the crowd as the assistants reappeared in the audience, unharmed. There was even a drama to the concessions sellers, who hawked their treats with booming voices and made cotton candy sound like a piece of cloud stolen from heaven. How could he leave it all behind?

When the audience was inside and settled, Harry picked up a mallet and beat a drum four times. He didn't have anyone to pull open a curtain, lower the lights, or play music for him, so this was the only way to make his entrance appropriately dramatic—or, at least, get the audience somewhat quiet for his entrance. He played one final drumroll and leaped onto the stage to a smattering of applause.

He started facing away from the audience. He stretched out his arms, and then, with a flourish, a fan of cards appeared in each hand. There was slightly more applause, and a boy hooted. Harry smiled to himself, gathering his confidence. The audience was his to win. With a deft move, he made the decks vanish again. He spun to face the crowd, and it felt like his stomach did a backflip.

He was there. In the front row.

Zoltan was relaxed in his seat, using a toothpick to remove dirt from under his fingernails. He glanced up at Harry, giving him the same expectant look as the rest of the audience. He was flanked by his two companions, Istvan and Bjorn.

The sight of the three men sent a shiver down Harry's spine. What were they doing just sitting there?

With nowhere to run, Harry had no choice but to start the show. Perhaps, if he could buy himself enough time, he'd come up with a plan. His mind raced as coins appeared and disappeared, handkerchiefs changed color, and cards obeyed his every command. Zoltan laughed at the appropriate moments, applauded for each successful trick, and was generally a perfect audience member.

He shouldn't have stayed in the city. He shouldn't even have gone back home. The only way to convince the Vespers he was dead would have been to disappear completely. Would they take it out on his family? Harry could imagine Zoltan and his companions walking up the stairs of the Weisses' house again, this time with murder on their minds.

But it was too late for recriminations now. Harry let the audience's applause build his confidence as he surprised a man by handing him the watch that had been on his wrist until a few minutes earlier.

Harry extended the show, buying himself time with elaborate stories and extra illusions. After the fourth card trick in a row, he could see a few audience members in the back begin filing out. If he didn't act soon, they would all leave, and he would be alone with the Vespers.

As soon as he'd made the decision, Harry felt his muscles relax. It was time to perform, and he was ready. Harry produced a new deck of cards and stepped off of the stage.

"Sir, would you please shuffle this deck for me?" he said, offering the cards to Zoltan, coming within an arm's length of the man who had tried to kill him. A part of Harry was screaming for him to make a run for it, but he buried it away.

It was showtime.

"Of course," Zoltan replied amiably, mixing the deck with the practiced ease of a gambler. Harry might have worried that the Vesper could stack the deck, but at this point he didn't care.

"Please take the first card for yourself," Harry said, letting his best announcer's voice boom through the tent as he stepped back onto the stage. "And pass the deck around. Ladies and gentlemen, each of you should take a single card from the deck.

"I will now present you with a new illusion. One that has never been seen before by mortal eyes!" he declared. There was no lie there—this was a trick that he had never even thought of before tonight. He walked to the center of the room and stood under the gas lamp. A successful magician would have drums and an orchestra to build the tension, but Harry only had the pounding of his heart against his rib cage.

"Examine your cards closely," he announced. "Look around—each of you has a different card. Now hold your card in the air, but hold it tightly." The audience complied, including an amused Zoltan. "I will turn out the light, and when I turn it back on, every one of you will have the exact same card," Harry announced.

He reached up to the lamp and turned the key, plunging the tent into darkness. Some of the ladies gasped, covering Harry's stealthy footsteps.

"Ladies and gentlemen!" he declared loudly.

"Brace yourselves!" He reached the door and began shaking the tentpoles.

"Prepare yourselves!" he boomed.

"I'm very sorry!" he shouted as he successfully pulled the tentpoles out, stepped through the door, and let the tent entrance collapse behind him as the audience screamed in shock.

It was a simple trick, really. Distract the audience with a big promise, turn out the lights . . . and then collapse the tent on them and run like the wind.

Harry broke into a sprint as he rounded the corner. The audience in the tent was yelling, but with a glance back, he confirmed that only part of the tent had collapsed. No one would be hurt.

No one but him. And, he realized with a sinking feeling, his family as well. Harry glanced back again. Zoltan and his crew had somehow made it out of the tent and were running after him.

They were fast, but Harry knew he was faster. He could put on a burst of speed and outrun them. But what was the point? He could run as far or as fast as he wanted, but the Vespers would find him. They were too connected. Too powerful. Too ruthless.

Harry knew the implicit threat that every criminal kingpin held over the more or less honest people that he preyed on. "Cross me, and I'll kill you. Run away, and I'll kill your family." Glancing back, he could see it written on Zoltan's face. Harry could run away and hide forever — but he couldn't hide his sick father. He couldn't hide his younger brothers and his little sister.

Harry stopped and turned around, letting the three Vespers catch up to him. He could see the fury on Zoltan's face, now modified with slight confusion.

Harry stood tall, facing the men, and held up his hands in surrender.

"Take me," Harry said. "I know it's over."

Istvan and Bjorn slowed, but Zoltan kept coming and lowered his shoulder. He slammed into Harry, knocking the wind out of him.

Harry's vision went blank for a moment and he

collapsed to the ground. His lungs burned as he strained for air. Harry gasped, but the breath just didn't seem to come.

"You don't get to negotiate with us," Zoltan said from above him. His two companions' laughter mingled with the roar of white noise in Harry's ears as he struggled for air.

For a moment, Harry was sure he would die, but ever so slowly his breath came back. Harry looked up at the three heads clustered above him, framed by the lights of the fairgrounds and the dim stars above that. No one would stop to question them. As far as Coney Island was concerned, large criminals had a right to beat up short boys. It wasn't worth risking their necks to interfere.

"Kill me," Harry croaked. "Only please, please, leave them alone."

Zoltan was unmoved. "You died last week when we threw you into the river. I even sent a telegram to Vesper One, telling him to add your drowning to my tally. I will *not* be made a liar." For that one moment, Harry thought he saw a flicker of concern in Zoltan's eyes. But then it was gone, and the ruthless killer was back. "Since the moment your feet hit the water, you've been living on borrowed time."

Harry closed his eyes. His escape had been for nothing. They were still going to kill him. They were still going to destroy his family. "But that's not how it has to be," Zoltan added. "You could be resurrected, if you do what needs to be done. How would you like to be alive again?"

Harry stared at Zoltan, unsure whether or not the man was playing a game with him. "What are you talking about?" he wheezed, still struggling to catch his breath after his sprint.

Zoltan inclined his head so he was looking straight into Harry's eyes. "You are a talented boy, even if you are a nosy piece of tenement trash. Your magician's tricks are not real artistry, but they have a certain utility." Harry bristled but remained silent. The more time this twisted criminal spent taunting him, the less time he'd have to torture Harry's family. "I need you to acquire an object for me. You'll break into the specified location, use your special *talents* to escape, and then bring me the item the day after tomorrow. I'll be waiting on the docks with a special crate to transport it back to Europe."

Zoltan leaned even closer. "If you succeed, I will forgive your family's debt and leave your father in peace. If you fail, you will be arrested and sent to prison for a long time. But don't expect anyone to visit you there—if you fail, I'll make sure each member of your family dies a unique and memorable death."

The Vesper rose, standing with the expansive performer's posture that Harry had worked so hard to imitate. "So do we have a deal?"

Harry didn't hesitate. He knew his parents would be horrified if they learned that he'd allowed the Vespers to pull him into their web of criminality and deceit, but there was no other choice.

"I'll do it."

Harry and Jacob shuffled through the crowd, doing their best to look like awestruck tourists. Given the unbelievable array of sculpture, pottery, and paintings around them, it wasn't difficult. There were paintings taller than Harry, full of knights, angels, and noble-women in vibrant colors. There was even a collection of daggers, swords, and armor with beautiful inlays. To Harry, the Metropolitan Museum of Art was like an elegant version of Coney Island, with all the drama and spectacle but none of the dirt, violence, and corruption. He and Jacob had worn their best clothes, but Harry still felt shabby next to the fine gentlemen and ladies taking the afternoon to stroll through the exhibits.

The museum was in an enormous brick building, topped with spires that made it look like a castle to Harry. And as large as it was, Harry had seen construction starting outside that looked like it would add entire new wings. Harry wished he could spend the day wandering through the museum. They'd even passed paintings by his famous ancestors, giving Harry a thrill that temporarily made him forget his nerves. But he had work to do—after memorizing the layout of the building, he had an even more important task:

locating the object the Vespers wanted him to steal.

On their way in, Jacob had purchased a map of the collections. Harry pretended to be confused, frequently pulling the map open and looking around in every direction. In reality, he was committing the entire map to memory. According to Zoltan, the plan called for him to be wheeled in during a fake delivery, and he couldn't know for sure where he would end up. He needed to be able to find his target from anywhere in the museum.

"Unbelievable!" Jacob whispered as they entered the Greek and Roman section, passing by a massive marble sarcophagus.

The plan was to sneak to the Greek and Roman exhibit, replace the artifact he was meant to steal with a replica the Vespers had created, and then deliver it to the Vespers' ship. Thinking about the assignment left Harry nauseous for a number of reasons. If he failed, his family would be punished in horrific ways. If he succeeded, a group of evil criminals would take a priceless treasure. But Harry knew what he had to do. When it came to choosing between his family and a piece of art — no matter how important — the choice was clear.

They strolled through the Greek and Roman exhibit casually, pretending to stop and examine every artifact. Harry could hardly believe that the statues, lamps, and even an incense burner had survived over two thousand years. He tried to imagine what relics might remain of his life in New York two thousand years from now. Would the tools for his magic tricks end up in a museum some day?

"Why did the Greeks need so many statues of head-less naked men?" Jacob asked, looking at a row of sculptures.

"According to this," Harry said, pointing to a plaque, "the head was probably broken off. But I don't know why these guys couldn't keep their clothes on."

Harry instinctively turned his head away and pulled out the map as a museum guard walked by. There was nothing to be worried about yet — the guard couldn't possibly know what they were planning — but he could feel himself tensing up anyway. He closed his eyes, stood up straight, and envisioned himself on stage. He was about to perform a routine disappearing act, nothing more. He opened his eyes and led Jacob to the target.

The artifact the Vespers wanted was tucked away in the corner of a room in the Greek and Roman wing of the museum. The gallery was full of marble statues and exotic figurines, busts of great leaders and ornate columns. But he was after a simple Hadra *hydria*, or water jar.

It looked like the small urns that the fortune-tellers in Coney Island used to decorate their tents and cultivate an air of foreignness, though less striking than those. Still, if the Vespers wanted it, the artifact had to be far more important than it appeared. The idea of Zoltan holding this work of art in his hands made Harry sick to his stomach.

It was locked in a glass case, and according to the plaque, it was from around 213 BC, and was inscribed with the name *Theudotos*, although scholars weren't sure why. Out of the corner of his eye, Harry examined the lock on the case and was relieved to discover that it looked fairly old. It wouldn't prove much of a problem. The locks on the doors to the museum were another matter entirely—Harry doubted that he could pick them quickly enough to avoid being caught. And worse, it had looked like they required a key to get either in or out.

Jacob nudged him. It was time to move on. A couple of poor boys in the museum were already an unusual sight—most of the other patrons were older gentlemen and well-dressed ladies.

"Why does he want it?" Jacob whispered as they walked on to the next case. "None of this makes sense."

Harry shook his head. "No idea. It's not really my concern, I guess. At least it's not one of those huge paintings—I have no idea how I would carry one of them out."

The boys wandered through the rest of the galleries, pretending to give the other artifacts just as much attention as they had paid to their target. A few minutes later, they sauntered out of the exhibit and headed back outside.

Harry would have preferred to scope out his escape

route, but it was off limits to the public. He would just have to trust that the Vespers' plan would work. As they walked out of the museum, Harry glanced back at the outside wall that he would need to rappel down on his way out. That would be after being smuggled in, making it past the night watchmen, and getting to the roof. The whole plan seemed to be one impossible feat stacked onto another, but he had no choice. The image of Zoltan stalking into Carrie's room was enough to strengthen Harry's resolve.

Harry parted ways with Jacob and headed for his rendezvous with the Vespers. It was time for the show.

Harry's legs were beginning to cramp. He was crammed into a large Egyptian urn, arms clutched tightly to his sides and head tucked down. A bag containing the replacement jug had been stuffed in on top of his head, and his knees banged into his chin every time the dolly transporting the urn hit a bump. The stairs up the front of the Metropolitan Museum had been the worst. "I'm supposed to be a demolitions expert, not a delivery boy," Bjorn had groused when Zoltan gave him this job. Harry was pretty sure Bjorn had bounced him straight up the steps out of spite.

They were lucky the vase hadn't come apart on those stairs. It was completely fake—the paint had barely dried by the time Harry climbed inside. Still, to his untrained eye, it had appeared real enough. He needed to believe the plan would work. If it failed, Harry would go to jail for attempted burglary and his family would be murdered. He wasn't sure whether it was the danger or the bouncing of the dolly that was making him feel sick.

The bumping finally came to a stop and Harry could hear voices through the urn's ceramic sides.

"Delivery for Egyptian art," Bjorn said in his thick Swedish accent. When they had been discussing the heist, Bjorn had suggested adding dynamite to Harry's crate so that he could set the fuse and run to the artifact, creating a diversion. Harry had been relieved when Zoltan vetoed the idea — especially since, judging by Bjorn's burned hair and lack of eyebrows, his methods didn't always work perfectly.

"Uh-huh," another man, probably a museum guard, said. "Do you have the bill of lading?"

There was a pause, and Harry's breath caught in his chest. He had known the plan was crazy, but he had expected to at least get into the museum before being arrested.

"Hmmmm. This is a little unusual." The guard's voice came through. "We weren't expecting this delivery today."

Bjorn mumbled something, too soft for Harry's ears.

Harry could hear someone opening the top of the shipping crate. A tiny bit of light filtered down around the uneven edges of the lid. Harry held his breath. All the museum guard had to do was lift off the lid, and the game would be up. Somehow Harry doubted that the museum could be convinced that a hidden Hungarian teenager was a standard feature of Egyptian urns.

Harry waited several long seconds as someone poked around at the packing materials.

"Well, all right, then," the guard said at last. "You'll find storage on the third floor, northeast corner. I'll show you the way. We're closing, so we'll have to be quick about it."

Harry breathed a sigh of relief as the crate was closed and the dolly began moving again. They bumped their way to the storage room on the third floor. To try to distract himself from the painful jostling, Harry counted each of Bjorn's footsteps and each turn they made. He called up an image of the floor plan of the museum, trying to track where they were headed. After eight turns, he started to lose certainty, but he still had a good enough idea to know which direction to head when he got out.

Finally, the crate was moved off of the dolly and placed on the ground. "Okay, let's get out of here," the guard said. "I need to lock up."

Harry heard two pairs of footsteps leave the room. A door closed and a key turned in the lock. As the sounds faded away, he could just make out the guard suggesting what landmarks Bjorn should visit while he was visiting New York City on his "delivery from Hungary."

Harry breathed deeply, waiting until he was sure

THE HOUDINI ESCAPE

129

they were completely gone. He listened, straining his ears for any signs that someone else was in the room with him. For a minute, he heard nothing, but then he heard the scratching of a pen piercing the silence.

Someone was in the room with him.

Harry waited. It could be a curator or restorer out there, finishing up some work. The museum might be closing, but the employees could easily stay for hours afterward. From time to time the employee would stand up, or move an object from one area to another. Harry was pretty sure his feet were asleep and his legs and arms with them, but there was nothing for it. He simply waited.

After what seemed like an hour, the man finished his work. Harry exhaled as the door opened and closed, and the key turned in the lock once again. He waited another ten minutes for good measure, then flexed his muscles and pushed out with his arms and legs. The cheap plaster holding the fake urn together cracked open inside the packing crate.

Careful not to harm the replica in the bag, Harry reached up and used his penknife to unhook the latch. After fumbling for a moment, it gave, and he was able to push the lid off and stand up.

He swayed as he stood, nearly falling over. He stood in place, balancing on the edges of the crate as he stamped his feet to restore feeling. Finally, he was able to gingerly climb out of the box. He cleaned up the materials that had fallen on the floor and closed the lid so that no one who happened in would notice something amiss.

The storeroom was filled with crates and tables covered with pieces of artifacts in the process of classification. There were sculptures, bowls, and even another urn. On one table lay a suit of armor, completely disassembled, surrounded by notes detailing plans to fit it back together. Soft light filtered in from high windows. Glancing up, Harry could see early evening stars.

Harry padded over to the door to see what he was up against. He had spent the last ten minutes planning how to pick this lock, trying to guess the type from the sound of the key the employees were using. But there was no obstacle. All he had to do was turn a small knob and he was ready to go.

It was almost a pity that he had to wait another hour until the last workers left and he could put the plan into action. Harry retired to a dark corner of the storeroom, hiding behind some empty crates and taking the opportunity to massage feeling back into his limbs.

Sitting in silence, he tried to shut out the worries that crowded his mind. What if he couldn't get to the Greek and Roman exhibit to take the artifact? He clutched the bag with the fake as images of Bjorn rigging his house with explosives hovered at the edge of his thoughts.

When he was confident enough time had passed, Harry exited the room and ghosted down the corridors, past the other storage areas and out into the Asian art exhibit. Occasionally he would hear or glimpse a guard, but he managed to slip into the Greek and Roman gallery unnoticed. In the darkness, the statues looked like silhouettes that might come to life at any moment to throw out the intruder stalking through their midst.

Harry found the water jug in its glass case, but that was no challenge. A lock pick hidden in Harry's belt made short work of it. He had just lifted the case open when he heard footsteps coming down the hallway outside. He laid the lid down delicately and slipped behind the case, crouching as low as he could. Had a guard heard him, or was it just a routine check?

As the guard came closer, the footsteps sounded like a clock ticking down the moments until Harry would doom his family to an early grave. Harry held his breath as the guard paused in the center of the room. The light from the guard's lantern played across the statues, casting the shadows of ancient heroes on the walls.

As the guard turned and headed out of the room, Harry exhaled. Working quickly, he opened the case and removed the jar. He opened the padded bag and pulled out the fake. Harry paused a moment, comparing the two side by side. Both bore the inscription of the Greek name, *Theudotos*.

It was staggering to Harry—two thousand years ago a Greek man had handled this same jar, likely even drank from it.

Harry couldn't imagine what Zoltan wanted with a simple terra-cotta jar. If it was money, there were famous paintings and sculptures in the museum that would sell for titanic sums on the black market. Harry examined the two objects more closely. They had handles on each side and faded black decorations painted around the tops.

The only difference between the two jars was that the real one had very faint scratches on the base. Was it an etching of a diagram of some sort? In the low light, he couldn't make anything out. The forger wouldn't have been able to see the base when he copied the vessel. Maybe it was just sloppy counterfeiting. Or was this what Zoltan was after?

Harry shook his head. Were the scratches on the urn a map to treasure, or to some more valuable artifact? It would just give the Vespers more resources to fuel their criminal enterprises. Whatever they were planning, all Harry could know for sure was that it would be something horrifying—and now he was their accomplice.

He cautiously placed the fake jar in the glass case and gently nested the real one in his padded bag. He used his lock pick to relock the case, and a moment later, he was gliding through the hallways of the museum.

As he passed by the Roman sarcophagus, light played over it from the opposite side. Harry crouched down and flattened himself against its base. He had been too distracted thinking about his escape, and hadn't noticed the guard returning. The sides of the sarcophagus were covered with figures of ancient

Romans, either writhing in pain or dancing. He didn't have time to look close enough to be sure—all he could tell was that their tiny limbs were uncomfortably jabbing him in the back.

The footsteps advanced and light spun around the shadow of the sarcophagus. The guard turned the corner, and Harry flattened against the marble, holding his breath and watching the guard stop and yawn. The lantern's light shined on the statues and urns—and Harry's blood froze as it turned toward him. Before he could move, the light landed squarely on Harry, and he heard the guard gasp.

Harry leaped up, and the guard lunged at him. The man's right hand brushed his shirt, but Harry danced away and the guard lost his balance for a moment and fell to the floor. Harry sprinted away as the man yelled.

"Intruder! Help! Intruder!" The guard's voice echoed through the empty hallways. Harry dodged a Roman chariot and darted out into the hallway. He could hear thudding footsteps and see lights coming from the Egyptian exhibit, so he charged into the Asian wing.

Woodcuts, paintings, pottery, and calligraphy blurred as he ran past. Twice he saw lights ahead of himself and changed course, scrambling down a different hallway. He could outdistance each individual guard, but they just kept coming. As he ran, he called up the map of the museum in his mind, trying to plot out a course that would avoid the known guards and get him where he needed to go.

Harry led the pursuit on a long loop around the building, dashing past massive paintings and what a sign said were Peruvian antiquities. Finally, when he was far enough ahead, he darted toward the curators' offices. He could hear the guards yelling behind him, but he skidded to a stop in front of the head curator's office. He tried the doorknob just in case, but he wasn't going to be so lucky. Pulling out his lock picks, he knelt and started on the knob.

He rotated the tumblers until he nearly had it, but his hands were shaking, and he accidentally pushed the locking mechanism back into place. The beating of his heart and the sound of advancing footsteps mingled in a terrifying drumbeat.

As the lock finally clicked open, he could hear guards turn the corner and advance down the hallway. Harry dashed inside and locked the door behind himself just as one of them slammed into it. With the exception of the fireplace, every wall of the office was lined with bookcases, and the large desk in the middle was covered with papers and even more books.

The guards started to pound on the entrance, and Harry could hear the jingle of keys on the outside as he pushed the curator's desk in front of the door. Just as it slid into place, he saw the knob turn.

The guards tried to open the door, but the heavy desk held it shut. Harry judged that it would keep them only for a minute. He stepped to the fireplace, nervously watching as the desk skid back and the door inched open.

Harry pulled a loop of thin rope out of his pocket and tied it around his waist, then to the straps of the bag, and set it just outside the fireplace, leaving a few feet of slack. Taking a deep breath, he jumped up and wedged himself into the chimney. He could barely make out a shaft of moonlight and stars at the top of the chimney.

Harry climbed up, pressing his back against one side of the chimney and his feet against the other. With his feet holding him steady, he put his hands back against the wall and pushed himself up. Then he worked his way up a few inches with his feet. Alternating back and forth, he made his way up the chimney. The rope pulled the bag up, and the artifact hung a few feet below him in the chimney. He could feel soot and ashes rubbing off all over his clothing and hair, with a sizeable portion sliding down the back of his shirt collar to his neck and back.

Below, he could hear the guards finally wrenching the door open. Harry just kept pushing himself higher, praying that if any of them looked up he would see only darkness. Finally, he reached the top and swung himself out onto the roof of the museum. He pulled the rope up, making sure not to knock the artifact in the bag. Once he had retrieved it, Harry slung the bag over his shoulders and headed for the front of the museum.

Harry coughed, trying to clear out the ashes choking

his lungs. The cool night air on the top of the museum was a relief from the sooty chimney. The roof was broad and open, with spires lining the edges before the shingles sloped down and met with the walls.

He looked out at the starlit street, watching a horse-drawn carriage carrying a laughing couple pass by. He hitched his rope to one of the spires and then climbed over the edge.

Harry braced his feet against the bricks, then jumped back and let out rope as he fell down. He grimaced as he swung back into the wall and his legs took the brunt of the impact. It would have been nice to rappel down slowly and easily, but he didn't have time. He pushed off again, bounding down the wall as quickly as he could.

Once down, he laid the rope against the wall and ducked down into the shadows of the building. Inside, he could hear guards shouting and could see lights playing on the windows, but no one seemed to have come outside yet.

While he waited for a horsecar carrying a load of workers home, Harry pulled a handkerchief from his pocket and used it to wipe most of the soot from his face and hair. Once the street was clear again, he set off, sticking to the shadows until he was several blocks away from the museum. Stepping into the light and quickening his pace, he headed for the docks.

An early morning fog was rolling in as Harry reached the East River. Most of the ships were tied up, dark, and silent, but the Vespers' steamship was a flurry of activity as three men used a winch and pulley system to load crates onto the ship.

Harry's heart was trying to claw its way out of his chest as he approached the three familiar figures standing on the pier. Zoltan's slick black hair gleamed in the light of the lanterns.

"It looks like the urchin may not be entirely worthless," Zoltan said with the grin of a predator. Harry felt a sudden urge to punch it off his face, but his looming accomplices made Harry think better.

"I've got it," Harry said. "That was my part of the deal. Will you leave my family alone?"

"I will — if it is genuine. Let me see it."

Harry felt every muscle in his body tighten. He was moments away from saving his family — if this criminal mastermind could be trusted. He pulled the bag off and handed it to Zoltan.

The Vesper gently extracted the Greek jar and held it out admiringly. "This will be perfect for my collection. Perhaps for holding water, or the ashes of an enemy. You know, I haven't cremated anyone alive yet. . . . Istvan, keep that in mind. I'm sure Bjorn can rig something up."

"Is the map still —" Zoltan shot Istvan a glance and he trailed off.

Harry wasn't sure who Theudotos was or what had

been inscribed on the jar, but he wished he could apologize to him for letting a Vesper handle his legacy. He hoped the Greeks would have understood why he did it and forgiven him.

Zoltan was nearly beaming as he walked over to the last crate on the pier. "Bjorn, help me open this. Istvan, please make sure that the boy doesn't leave us just yet."

Istvan's heavy hand fell on Harry's shoulder. He wanted to shove it off and run, but he simply stood silently and watched them pack the artifact away. The interior of the crate was constructed to hold this object—it was full of padding material but included a special spot for the artifact. Harry could barely imagine what would make this inscription so valuable, but the thought of the Vespers controlling it made his stomach twist.

Zoltan snapped his fingers at Bjorn. "This is to go at the very bottom of the hold. Put a guard on it at all times," he instructed. "No one opens it until it reaches Vesper One. We can't afford to disappoint him." There was that same flicker of uncertainty, momentarily breaking through Zoltan's poised exterior.

Harry looked into the distance, catching a glimpse of movement in the fog.

"There's no one coming to help you," Istvan growled.

Zoltan turned and shouted to the men on board the ship. A few seconds later, two appeared on the rails and began hauling. They pulled the crate into the air and deftly landed it on the deck.

With the ship loaded, Zoltan spun and focused his attention on Harry. "You've put on a good show. But the audience demands the finale it was promised. You're coming with us."

Harry's insides twisted. Istvan tried to pull him forward, but he jerked back. For a moment, Istvan's grip was broken, and Harry made to run. But he only managed to take two steps before Zoltan slammed into him, and Harry was on the ground with a blade at his throat.

"You're coming, or your family pays the price. Understand?"

The urge to fight evaporated. Harry nodded slightly, the steel at his throat leaving him unable to speak.

Zoltan stood, with a satisfied smirk on his face.

Istvan and Bjorn hauled Harry to his feet. Despite their grips on his arms, Harry drew himself up to his full height—even if it was half a foot shorter than the men around him.

"If it means my family lives, I'll come with you."

Zoltan smiled with satisfaction and turned to head up the gangway. Istvan and Bjorn kept a tight grip on Harry's arms as he followed.

The three men on the deck smirked at Harry as he was dragged on board. Zoltan beckoned for Istvan to follow him below deck, leaving Harry with Bjorn and his only slightly less menacing companions.

Their backs were facing the crate they were meant to be guarding, and Harry whispered a silent word of thanks before taking a deep breath and shouting, "Police!"

His stage training paid off. The Vespers all dashed toward the railing before turning back to Harry with cold fury in their eyes. "There's no one there," Bjorn snapped, grabbing hold of Harry's arm again.

And there wasn't. The only sounds were the grunts of the Vesper crewmen as they moved the crate toward the hold, and the thud of Harry's rapidly beating heart.

Harry stood at the back of the ship, watching the city recede. He tried to fix the skyline in his memory. This might be the last time he saw it.

The deck creaked as Zoltan approached. Harry turned to face the Vesper, standing straight and looking him in the eye.

"I killed you before," Zoltan began. He leaned back against the rail, utterly at ease.

Harry waited, trying to match the Vesper's deadly calm. But he could feel his chest fluttering with every breath he pulled in.

". . . but you're not dead," the Vesper added.

"Your powers of observation are impressive," Harry said, thankful that his voice didn't betray the fear welling up inside of him. "I got you the artifact," he continued. "I expect you to uphold your end of the deal."

Zoltan shook his head. "You did well, for a

gutter-trash trickster. But I'm afraid I sent a telegram saying that you drowned. I don't lie to Vesper One, so I have to remedy this . . . inconsistency." He sighed. "And you know far too much about our mission here. Did you really think we'd let you go, with what you've seen?" Zoltan stood up from the rail. "The audience needs the ending that they were promised. The show must go on."

Although every muscle in his body twitched with the need to run, Harry remained still as Istvan and Bjorn advanced on him. Within moments, his hands were chained behind his back.

"This time he'll stay down there," Istvan grunted.

"Should we attach a little dynamite for good measure? Maybe throw a hand grenade after him?" Bjorn asked eagerly as he fastened cuffs on Harry's legs, attached to a heavy metal ball.

Zoltan tilted his head to the side as if considering the proposal. "No, it's not necessary. We should save the explosives in case the coast guard decides to pay us a call. Just stick with the original plan."

Harry looked out across the water. The steamship was gliding along the water, and the docks were starting to disappear in the distance. The lights of Manhattan gleamed in the early-morning darkness as the night shift returned home and workers kissed their families good-bye and headed to their jobs.

Bjorn shoved Harry to the ground and he groaned as they stuffed him — manacles, chains, ball, and all—into a burlap sack. The cold of the metal on his arms and legs felt like the grip of death itself, ready to pull him down to a forgotten grave on the bottom of the bay.

"You promised you wouldn't hurt my family," Harry said, fixing Zoltan with a glare. The Vesper had gone back on his word once already—his promise was worthless. Harry tried to banish the thought of his feeble father being thrown to the ground, but the terrible image only grew more vivid.

"I did. And since you got us the artifact, they're no longer worth my concern. They'll live out their insignificant little lives," Zoltan said as the sack closed and the sliver of starlit sky narrowed. Harry's breathing was quick and shallow, and he clenched his fists, digging his nails into his palms in a futile attempt to keep panic at bay.

The men started to drag him to the railing. He struggled, trying to slow them down as best he could. He needed to buy time while his hands frantically felt for the lock on the chain that bound him. He started yelling as they hoisted him up to the rail. The weight of the ball chained to his feet nearly broke his ankle before someone grabbed it and pulled it up.

His stomach lurched as he spun in freefall.

Harry took a huge breath as he fell, filling his lungs with precious air. His earlier stuggle paid off and the lock on his hands gave way just as he was hitting the water. He'd bought himself just enough time to pick the lock on his handcuffs. But the heavy weight was still attached to his legs, and he was sinking straight down.

Harry struggled in the water, his movements slowed by chains, burlap sackcloth, and the cold all around him. His penknife slashed at the burlap fabric, but to his horror, it didn't seem to give. Finally, he pierced the sack and managed to claw his way out. He dropped the knife and grabbed for the shredded fabric. If the material floated to the surface, the Vespers would know he was trying to escape.

Harry looked up through the murky water, trying to stay calm as his air supply rapidly diminished. He could still see the hull of Zoltan's ship, its steam-powered paddle pushing it forward with considerable speed. It was already too far away for him to catch. There would be no hiding on the other side of the ship this time.

With a dull thump, the ball landed on the floor of the harbor. Harry reached down and quickly picked the lock on the manacles around his ankles. His body floated upward, but by holding the ball and chain he stayed at the bottom.

His lungs were burning, but he had to stay down a little longer. He watched as the hull of the Vesper ship moved farther out into the harbor. His brother Theo had once timed him at two minutes and fifty seconds with his head underwater, but at this depth it felt like he was being crushed.

Harry watched bubbles escape his nose and float to the surface, his vision beginning to blur. He needed to head for the surface, but he also needed to stay down until the ship was far enough away. If they saw he was alive, the trick would be up. This was the show. He had to fool them completely, or they would come back and take revenge on his family.

Harry clenched his fists around the chain, willing himself to stay calm. He was the King of Cards, the Prince of the Air, and a master escape artist. He could hold his breath for a few more precious seconds.

Finally, he started to see red behind his eyelids. Harry let the chain slip out of his grasp and kicked off, struggling for the surface. As he reached the top, he slowed, letting only the front of his face break through. The ship was far away now, but it was possible that they were still looking back for him. Harry breathed in, pulling in as much air as he could. He panted for a moment, letting his vision return to normal, and then he kicked his legs and dove back underwater.

With powerful strokes, he swam in the opposite direction of the ship, staying underwater as much as possible. An observer would have to look at just the right moment to see a mouth and nose emerge above the surface for a quick breath, then disappear again.

Harry glanced back at the ship and saw it rounding the shoreline before finally disappearing. He treaded water for a moment to catch his breath, and then set off for the shore at a more leisurely pace.

Harry met Jacob at the pier, just as they had planned. Harry pulled himself out of the water and stood up, shaking the water out of his hair. "How did it go?" he asked, struggling to catch his breath.

Jacob was grinning like a maniac. "Your plan worked perfectly." He handed Harry the parcel.

Harry took the artifact, hardly believing he was holding it once again. After the events of the past few days, it seemed miraculous that he'd managed to fool the Vespers. But Jacob had managed to climb up from underneath the docks, and as they'd discussed, swap the urns while Harry created a distraction. They knew it was a long shot, but it had actually worked.

"I owe you," Harry said, smiling. He knew from his reading that no great magician, not even the great Robert-Houdin, had pulled off his act alone. It paid to have a best friend who was skilled in his own right.

Jacob raised an eyebrow. "That's not all. While I was up there, I . . . got a little greedy." He passed Harry a second parcel, this one a simple leather case. Harry opened it and gasped.

"How did you . . . ?"

"This was next to the artifact I switched. It must be their blackmail money, or something."

Harry laughed. It was a good thing Zoltan wouldn't discover that anything was missing until he was in the middle of the Atlantic Ocean. Inside the case was more money than Harry made in a year. He knew immediately what they would use it for. It was enough to take care of his family while he and Jacob finally created the act they had dreamed of. As soon as he returned the artifact to the museum—an anonymous parcel mysteriously appearing in the night watchmen's room would do the trick—he could start planning.

Harry shivered, this time more with excitement than with cold. His real life was about to start.

The audience clapped as Harry leaped onstage and took a bow. The large tent was packed for the third show in a row. Their statewide tour, word of mouth, and the posters touting their stage name, "The Brothers Houdini," had brought the Harlem hometown crowd out in force. Harry and Jacob had showcased their best illusions, from simple card and scarf tricks to an elaborate "mind reading" act. Now it was time for the finale.

Tonight wasn't just any show. In the front row, Harry could see his mother, his brothers, and his sister. Even his father, who could barely walk, had been wheeled down so that he could watch. Mayer Samuel's face was thin and taut, but Harry could detect a slight smile on it. His father still didn't entirely approve of his son's new venture, but Harry had caught him looking around at the crowd in wonder more than once.

As Jacob invited the local constable onstage, Harry

looked down at the orchestra, a four-piece band that he had recently hired. What a difference it made having music to build tension! Together Jacob and the constable put Harry in handcuffs and leg irons, and tied a generous portion of rope around him. Just before they pulled a bag over his head, Harry flashed the crowd his most winning smile.

They led Harry to the crate and he crouched down, letting them guide him inside. The audience clapped as the front slammed shut and Jacob snapped a heavy padlock into place.

Harry couldn't see a thing, but he knew what was happening outside. The orchestra was starting up, high fast notes building the excitement — and masking the sounds that Harry was making. Jacob would be joking with the crowd and making sure they knew that the constable wasn't a plant. The cuffs and leg irons were the real deal.

Next, Jacob would produce a sheet and wave it about. He would climb onto the top of the box and hold it out with both hands, shielding himself from the audience. The orchestra would reach a crescendo as he lowered it down just enough to show his head one last time. Then in one smooth motion he would fling the sheet aside.

Only it wasn't Jacob anymore. The metamorphosis appeared instantaneous, and Harry stood in his place, grinning at the audience once again. The money they'd taken from the Vespers had allowed them to design the most impressive trick anyone in Coney Island had ever seen.

The crowd erupted in applause, and Harry jumped down on the stage, taking a bow. With the constable's help, he unlocked the front of the box and helped out Jacob, who was wearing the cuffs, leg irons, rope, and a sack over his head. The audience roared its appreciation and the constable smiled in amazement and shook his head as he used his key to let Jacob free.

Harry and Jacob clasped hands, walked to the front of the stage, and took a bow as the audience applauded. After another bow, they backed up and the curtain drew shut.

But the crowd wasn't done. "HOU-DI-NI, HOU-DI-NI," they chanted. Harry peered through the side of the curtain. Even his father was shouting it.

He locked eyes with Jacob and shrugged. They could do one more trick, couldn't they? After a quick discussion, they settled on a new illusion that Harry had invented a few weeks ago, and they had been practicing ever since. Jacob grabbed their props from stage left and Harry signaled for the stagehand to raise the curtain again.

The stagehand yanked the rope and the curtain slid open. Harry Houdini stepped into the light, ready to amaze his audience one more time.

THE SUBMARINE JOB

PART 3

Connecticut, 1955

Fiske Cahill was going to drown.

Water filled his nose and mouth and eyes, and all he could do was flail his arms and pray it would stop soon. The world around him was a dull roar, muffled by the sound of the water as it flooded his ears. The hand on the back of his head held him still; there was no escape.

Suddenly, it jerked him backward. He gasped in the air, even though it smelled like bleach and too-sweet air freshener. He could taste the chemicals in the air and he spat, trying to keep the water from trickling down past his lips.

"Come on, now," said the boy behind him. "I thought you were a fish. Aren't you a fish, Fish Face?"

"No," Fiske grunted before his face was shoved back into the toilet. He only barely snapped his mouth closed in time. Faintly, he could hear the last bell of the day ringing from the hallways. Like dogs at the sound of a whistle, the boys let go of Fiske. He threw himself backward, away from the toilet. The group around him, four or five boys from the years ahead of him, backed away, laughing. They all sucked their cheeks in and put their hands to their necks, waving their fingers like gills as they ran out of the bathroom. Their leader, Eric Landry, turned on the faucet before he left, flinging water at Fiske with his fingertips.

It was not a good way to end the day.

Fiske pulled himself up off of the wet, slippery bathroom floor and went to the sink. His hair was soaked and so was his sweater, from his shoulders down to his stomach. Drops of toilet water trickled down over his ears and nose. Fiske grabbed desperately for a fistful of brown paper towels and scrubbed at his face and hair.

It was utterly mortifying, even with no one else in the bathroom.

This sort of thing should not happen to Fiske Cahill. It shouldn't happen to a Cahill at all.

He picked his books up from the corner where Eric and his gang of friends had thrown them. His history book was splayed open with its papery guts shown to the world. George Washington stared back up at him, sword raised, horse rearing. He was willing to bet that George Washington never got swirlied. Or that Shakespeare never had a note reading "Kicketh me" taped to his back, or that Mozart never had his sheet music pitched into the toilet. Fiske was supposed to have something in common with such amazing people. They were his cousins, after all, all of them far-flung members of the Cahill family. The Cahills—the most powerful family in the history of the world. Cahills were supposed to be something special, untouchable. They were supposed to be great.

Some good that was doing for Fiske. The only thing he was great at was distracting Eric and his friends from their homework.

Fiske tucked his books into his backpack and stepped into the main hall at school. He'd be able to go home for the summer soon, he told himself. It was early May, so there was only a month left of school. He could last a month.

Outside, the spring sun was hot and groups of his schoolmates lounged around on benches or threw a football across the green. It was a beautiful campus, made of lush lawns against stately brick buildings with white columns in front of them. But Fiske kept his head down as he crossed toward the dorms, and so he didn't see very much of it.

"Fiske Cahill! Mr. Cahill!"

One of the secretaries was hailing him, waving a piece of paper in the air. "Fiske Cahill, don't make an old lady run across the lawn. Come here, and be quick about it!"

Fiske looked up and around him. Were they all staring at him now? Oh, no. Fiske hurried across the lawn, feeling his ears and neck burn bright red with embarrassment.

"Why are you all wet?" asked the secretary, wrinkling her nose at him.

"Uh," said Fiske, and then he mumbled something about a water fountain.

"A telegram for you," said the secretary, handing it over. Her fingernails were painted scarlet to match her bright red sweater. "An emergency, it says. Silly, if you ask me. It doesn't make any sense! Well, not that I meant to read your private business or anything, but I had to make sure it wasn't anything bad or illegal." She looked at him from over her half-moon eyeglasses in a way that made him feel as if he were beneath a swinging lamp in an interrogation room.

"Y-yes, ma'am," he said, unfolding the telegram.

"And here I am, running across the whole school to deliver your nonsensical telegram. Let me tell you, if I wanted to deliver messages I would have been born a carrier pigeon. Well? Are you going to say thank you, young man?"

"Uh, thank you," said Fiske, glancing up from the telegram for only a moment. The secretary frowned at him, then turned quite sharply and marched back to the office, likely muttering something about kids these days.

FAMILY TROUBLE STOP. NEW YEAR'S 1946 STOP. OLD FAMILY FRIENDS EVERYWHERE STOP. GRACE.

Fiske could only stare at the telegram, his stomach going cold and his mouth dry. It looked like a simple note to anyone else, but Fiske could see through the lines. Family trouble. Grace was in trouble.

Old family friends everywhere.

Vespers. Sworn enemies of the Cahills.

New Year's 1946? Fiske's mind was clicking so rapidly that it was having trouble making complete thoughts. For Christmas 1945, he'd gotten a new set of watercolors and a brand-new easel. He could remember that. Grace had given them to him. And then he hadn't been allowed to stay and paint things because — because why?

Because they'd had to go to Washington, DC. There had been Cahill business to attend to, and no one would let Fiske stay home when the nanny was visiting her sister. So Grace was in Washington.

Surrounded by Vespers.

Fiske folded the telegram again and shoved it in his pocket. He was shaking so hard that he thought his skin would come loose and fall off; his breath was so strained in his throat that he might choke on the air. Grace wouldn't have risked sending a message to school if she wasn't in danger. He glanced around again; was anyone still looking at him? Had they even been looking in the first place? Cahill business made him uncomfortable — vulnerable, as if he was being watched.

With one more stealthy look around, Fiske turned

straight for the headmaster's office. He'd have to get permission to leave as soon as possible.

And then he ran into something. Or someone. Eric Landry.

"What have you got there, Fish Face?" Eric asked, holding out his hand.

Fiske only looked at him. *Not now*, he screamed inside his head. *Get out of the way.*

"Now what have you got there that's got you so long in the face?" asked Eric, making a grab for Fiske's pocket. "Girlfriend break up with you? Your dog die? Gramma fallen sick, Fish Face? Someone snatch her up and ship her back to the sea? Your gramma is a fish, too, isn't she? A big old whale, maybe?"

"Don't rip it!" Fiske yelped, the words squeaking out of him as if he had been squeezed too hard. He jerked away, holding the telegram tightly.

"Oh, don't rip it!" Eric sang, mocking Fiske. He made another grab for it. Fiske jumped out of the way. "Stop moving around, Cahill, and give me that telegram."

"Hey, Eric," said one of the other boys. "Let him go. He looks upset."

"He's gonna look more upset if he doesn't cough up that telegram."

"Why do you care?" said the other boy. His name was Matthew, and he was in Fiske's history class. "It's nothing important. It's just Cahill. Like anything exciting or interesting would ever happen to him."

Fiske held his breath. He needed to go; he needed to get out of this.

Eric smirked at Matthew and then shoved Fiske away. "Get out of my way, Cahill."

Fiske turned on his heel and ran off toward the headmaster's office. Eric and Matthew and the other boys laughed as he sprinted away.

George Washington would never, ever run away from anything. Something burned in Fiske at the thought. Something that said no matter how he tried, he'd never live up to the standards that he was supposed to meet.

In the headmaster's office, the secretary in bright red lifted an eyebrow at him. "You know the rules. You can't just *leave* school."

"B-but I have to go," said Fiske, showing her the telegram. "It's from my sister. If there's a family emergency, I need to be there for it." He wet his lips and shifted from foot to foot. They *had* to let him go.

"That's very touching," said the secretary, pushing the telegram back toward him. "But I'm afraid the headmaster isn't available at the moment. And look, it says right there that you have old family friends all over the place. That's nice, isn't it? Your sister isn't alone."

"It's, uh, it's not the same as family," said Fiske. "Please, can't I see him? He'll understand, I know he will."

"No. I'm afraid he's not here at the moment. So sorry about that. But you can schedule an appointment with him for next Wednesday."

"But that's over a week from now!" said Fiske, his voice cracking. "If it's an emergency, then I need to leave right away."

"I'm so *very* sorry for the inconvenience, but I'm afraid that's the best I can offer you," said the secretary. She smiled at him then, and it wasn't a very nice smile at all. It was the kind of smile a cat would give a canary right before gobbling it down.

Fiske wanted to throw things. He wanted to jump up onto her desk and pitch a fit and force her to see that this wasn't a game. It wasn't something silly. It was a Cahill thing, and more than that, it was *Grace*.

Instead, he bit his tongue and ran out of the office. He would go to his dorm. He would figure something out. Somehow.

The secretary waited until he was gone, and then picked up the phone. With her red fingernails, she spun the rotary dial, waiting impatiently as it ticked back and forth.

"Yes, hello," she said. "This is Eighty-nine. The Boy King will be trying to flee soon. I've tried to delay him, but he'll take alternative measures. I'm recommending a tail, and eyes at Meriden and the train station.

Very good. Thank you." She put the receiver down and picked up a nail file.

The door to the headmaster's office opened, and he stuck his head out. "Did I just hear a student out here, Marilyn?"

"No, of course not. There's nothing to worry about, sir," she said. "Nothing to worry about at all."

In his dorm room, Fiske pulled a bag from beneath his bed. Grace had told him to always keep one packed. He'd rolled his eyes when she said it, but as a Cahill, he didn't really have a choice in the matter. He pulled off his damp sweater and changed into a clean black one. Outside, the sun was falling down behind the trees. It wouldn't be fully dark for a few more hours, but he didn't have that kind of time. He'd have to go now.

Fiske put his ear to the door; in the hall, boys were heading to dinner or to study. He could say he was going to the library, but the library was closed during dinner and everyone knew that. He could say he was headed to the field houses, but no one would believe that.

On his dresser was a framed photograph, taken last Christmas. Fiske was in the corner, per usual, looking awkward and half hidden in shadow. His father, a stern-faced and silent man, sat on a chair in the center of the frame. His sister Beatrice was beside him, a smile pressed into her face so unnaturally it was as if someone had to arrange her mouth and chin just to show her how it might work. And then there was Grace, beaming and full of so much life that she practically made the picture move. She was turned toward him, her arms outstretched, trying to pull Fiske into the forefront. Grace was twelve years older than him, but he had never felt any distance between the two of them. They weren't much, that family. They were fractured and imperfect. Two of them, actually, were rather dysfunctional and not very nice. But they were still his.

He picked up the frame and gazed at it for a moment longer.

Fiske glanced behind him. There was always the window.

He threw the curtains back and lifted the sash. There was no one below, but he was still two stories from the ground. He looked at his watch; the dinner bell would ring soon.

With a grunt, Fiske threw his bag out the window toward the trees. It landed with a crash in the underbrush, and he winced at the noise. But it didn't seem that anyone heard it. So hopefully no one would notice the freshman climbing out of the window, either.

Doing something he once read about in a book, Fiske took the sheets off of his bed and knotted them together. It didn't seem like a very long rope, and it looked even shorter by the time he'd tied a corner of it to his dresser. People in his books must have more bedclothes than he did. Still, he threw the end of his sheet rope out the window.

And there were still a good seven or eight feet between the end of it and the ground.

He climbed onto the windowsill and wrapped his legs around the sheets. The dresser wobbled a bit as he slowly edged his way down the homemade rope. The sheets began to slip their knots. Fiske wavered, his arms and legs shaking so hard that he could have been the victim of the world's tiniest earthquake. He tried to scramble down before the sheets fell or the dresser toppled out the window, but it didn't work. He lost his grip, and before he understood what was happening, Fiske's arms and legs were flailing through nothing but air. He landed on his back, and all of the breath flew out of him.

It took a minute of lying there in the bushes and grass to get his breath back, but he jumped up as soon as he could. Now what? The airport was a good five miles away, at least.

Beyond the tree line was a row of faculty houses, residences specifically set aside for teachers with families. And there, leaning against a back porch, was a bicycle with streamers on the handlebars and a pink plastic basket.

Of course, he thought. *Of course it would be an eight-year-old girl's bike.* It couldn't be a moped or something cool.

He swung his leg over the pink banana seat,

mentally promised the little girl that he'd get the bike back to her, and then sped off down a service road.

But there was someone waiting for him there.

The secretary stood in the middle of the street, her hands on her hips and a very disapproving look on her face.

"I should have known you would try to sneak away. It's incredibly rude to do something when you've been told you don't have permission."

"How did you know that I—how—I'm, I'm sorry," said Fiske. "But I have to go."

"Oh, to your sister. I know, darling boy. But you really shouldn't worry about her. She's with some friends of mine, and they're just dying to talk to her." The secretary smiled in that not-very-friendly way of hers.

Fiske felt as if he had been washed in snow. The secretary's friends? There was a Vesper working at his school?

"We're everywhere, Mr. Cahill," said the secretary. "Don't think that we're not. Now, I know you're a good boy. You'd much rather be sketching your family tree than trying to live up to it and never doing so, am I right? Of course I am. So, get off the bicycle. Let your sister put out her own fires. And perhaps you'll live to see another day."

A part of Fiske crumbled, like a piece of a cliff tumbling down into the sea. He stared at the secretary with her red suit, her gray hair curled into a little iron helmet.

He put his foot back on the pedal.

The secretary lifted a finger. "I'm giving you a chance. You're a snotty little Cahill, but you're just a boy. The others won't be as forgiving. The others would kill you as soon as they looked at you, Fiske Cahill. Don't think they don't know where you're going, or who you'll see."

Fiske pushed off. He tried to gain as much speed as he could, whipping past the secretary. She yelled out at him, turning and chasing him down the road. Her scarlet claws grabbed at the back of his sweater, but he sped away.

He didn't want a chance to turn around. He didn't want to be delayed. He knew that the secretary would run back to her desk and call whoever it was that she had to call, but he couldn't worry about any of that right now. He needed to get to Grace, and they would handle it together.

He had a sister to save.

Meriden was the nearest airport, and while it was ten minutes away by car, it took considerably longer to get there through the wooded paths at dusk, on a small girl's bicycle. Fiske didn't dare use the main road.

There were some old paths through the forest that some of the older boys used when they were sneaking out; Fiske followed one of those. His teeth clattered against one another from fear and from the cold.

He didn't have a lot of time; he knew the Vespers would be waiting, looking for him. They could be crawling all over the small airport in the quickly falling darkness.

The airport was sleepy and dark when he arrived at the security gate. The watchman was napping, but he opened his eyes when Fiske rapped on the window.

"I need to use the Cahill plane," he said. "It's an emergency."

The security guard wiped his nose and buzzed Fiske onto the airport grounds. The Cahills had kept a plane at Meriden and a pilot on retainer. He was available at any hour that Fiske or Grace might need him. This was another family precaution that Fiske had huffed and moaned about, but Grace's choices were becoming more and more clear. Everything was about the Clue hunt — whether Fiske agreed with that set of priorities or not. He bit his lip. It wasn't fair to think that way, but he couldn't help it.

Fiske rode his bike to the hangar. Pete, the pilot, was wiping down the Cahill plane's nose with a cloth. Pete had been in dogfights in World War II. The danger had made him nearly fearless, but possibly a bit crazy. Which, in turn, made him an excellent Cahill ally.

"Well, hey there, young Cahill," said Pete. "Thought I wouldn't be seeing you until the end of term."

"F-family emergency," said Fiske. "I need to go to Washington, DC. Right — right away."

"Right away, eh? Glad you made it here now; a few minutes more and I'd be having myself some dinner."

"I'm sorry to keep you from your dinner, Pete, but it really can't wait. Not another minute."

"Well, then. Good thing we've got peanuts on board. Go ahead and get yourself all settled there. I'll get the garage door up here and we'll be off like a flash."

"Thank you, Pete," said Fiske, pulling the plane's door open and climbing in.

It was a small airplane—a two-seater cockpit with four seats in the cabin—not something that Fiske would really trust to take him across the ocean, or really any farther than the Great Lakes. But from Connecticut to Washington, or Connecticut to home, it was okay. And quick. Fiske put his bag in the cabin, but climbed into the cockpit beside Pete's captain's chair. He didn't want to sit alone—it seemed rude.

Pete had the hangar door up and the engines on in record time, and soon they were taxiing out to the small runway.

"How's landing at Hyde for you, young Cahill?" asked Pete.

"That's fine, thanks," said Fiske. He was staring out the window. A pair of headlights was on the runway. "Pete, are cars allowed on the runway?"

"Nope," said Pete, checking his gauges and dials from the cockpit. "Not usually, at least. 'Less it's a maintenance crew or something like that." Pete and Fiske squinted at the headlights. They looked like they were coming straight toward the plane.

"Pete, let's go!" Fiske said. An uncomfortable thought had lodged itself in his imagination, and it wasn't going to let go. "We've got to go before they get here."

"If someone's on the runway—and good golly, they are—we can't take off. We'll run into them. And that won't end well for anyone," said Pete, lifting his eyebrows.

That's when there was a flash and a *pop*.

"They're shooting at us," Fiske said, his panic growing like a balloon about to burst. "Oh, holy pancakes, they're shooting at us. Pete, we have to go!"

"They're shooting at us!" Pete yelled, his gaze darting nervously between the view through the windshield and the gauges in the cockpit.

"They're shooting at us, Pete, they're shooting at us! Go, go faster!" Fiske yelled. He felt as if he were climbing and clawing the cockpit. There was another flash and another *pop*, and Fiske covered his eyes, as if that would keep him from dying.

The airplane's engines roared to full power. Pete pulled back on the throttle, and the plane began to move.

"Go, Pete, go faster!"

"I'm going fast! I'm going as fast as physics lets me!" Pete yelled.

Fiske glanced over at his pilot—Pete's teeth were clenched together and a bead of sweat was making his way down his face. They were going faster and faster, and the car was nearer and nearer.

"Hope your seat belt is on, young Cahill!" said Pete. He pulled on the steering wheel and they pointed upward. Fiske looked out the side of the cockpit, and he saw men in the car — he saw their faces, their guns. The plane lifted, but too slowly. The fuselage shuddered and jerked as the back landing gear scraped the top of the car. Fiske was thrown around like a doll; his seat belt locked and so his head flew forward, his elbow jammed into the windshield. The plane wobbled like it was balanced on the head of a pin, and the popping continued below.

They weren't even going to make it off the runway. Fiske's emergency trip would be over before it even started. Pete was yelling something in French — probably something he'd picked up in the war — and all Fiske could do was hold on to whatever was at hand.

And then, the jerking stopped. The air around them was smooth. The plane wasn't falling out of the sky.

"That was a close one there, wasn't it?" said Pete, grinning. "We should do that more often. That's a good kind of flying! Makes me feel like a younger man, you know. Back in the war again. Ah, that's some good kind of flying!"

Fiske collapsed back into his chair and let out the breath he had been holding. Hopefully the rest of his adventure would go smoothly.

The Willard Hotel was an unofficial Cahill institution. Practically across the street from the White House, it could be argued to be the real seat of power in the country. It was a rare day when there wasn't at least one Cahill checked in.

Grace Cahill had spent many a day and night there. She didn't think she had ever been so frightened, though.

She was pacing, checking the peephole of her hotel room every few minutes. Her nerves were standing on end, and a black swirl of dread circled around in her chest. She shouldn't have sent that telegram. She should have found a way out on her own. But, as unwilling as Grace was to admit it, she was terrified, in over her head. She hated to drag her little brother into this mess, this pit of vipers and fire. But she didn't have a choice.

Grace checked the peephole again and then the window. He should be here by now. Fears and what-ifs breathed down her neck like unhappy ghosts. Suppose they'd caught up with him. Suppose they'd captured him, delayed him, were planning on using him as bait to lure her out. Perhaps they'd done worse—

She stopped her pacing and pressed her palms against her closed eyes. *It doesn't do any good to think like that. It doesn't do any good to do anything but hope.*

She glanced at the clock on the nightstand. Grace

tried to remind herself that not everything happened on a smooth timetable. There could have been any number of small obstacles that came up. Still, it was getting late.

There was a knock, and Grace flew to the door, peering out the peephole. Fiske stood on the other side. But was it really Fiske? Had he been followed? She hated, sometimes, that her life made her doubt even the plainest of facts.

"Who's there?" Grace demanded.

"It's me," he said. "It's Fiske."

"When's your birthday?"

"March 31, 1941," said Fiske. "Let me in, Grace."

"No," said Grace. "That was too easy. What's your favorite animal? What's my favorite animal?"

"Mine is a giraffe," said Fiske. "Yours is a dragon. Which, you know, isn't even a real thing. Let me in!"

"What color is the carpet in the second-floor music room at home?"

"Grace!" he half shouted, half hissed. "Well, it used to be white. And then I spilled that green paint on it, so now it's kind of . . . spotted. And I said I was sorry about that, by the way. There's no need to keep bringing it up. Grace, come on and let me in."

Satisfied, Grace slid the chain lock open, turned the deadbolt, opened the door, and grabbed her brother by the collar. She dragged him in and immediately shut the door after him, sliding and turning all of the locks back into place.

"Grace, why is it so dark in here?" asked Fiske. The curtains were pulled against the night, and the only lamp on was a small reading light that Grace had put on the floor.

"They know I'm here," she said, peeking out of the peephole again. "How did you know what room I was in?"

"I asked for Miss Edith at the front desk," said Fiske. It was their mother's name, and a good pseudonym. Fiske watched Grace with nervous eyes. He'd never seen her so scared before.

"Right," said Grace. She took a towel from the bathroom and stuffed it along the crack at the bottom of the door.

"Grace? Grace," Fiske said, but she didn't look up. "Grace!" Fiske grabbed her arm and only then did she stop, turning to him with the most anxious expression he'd ever seen. "What's going on?" asked Fiske. "You're scaring me. You need to just . . . to just sit there, okay? Just sit down." He helped to ease her down onto the corner of one of the beds and then perched on the corner across from her. "We'll be okay for five minutes, right?"

"I don't know," she said. "They've never been this close before, Fiske. Not to me. I can feel them—I can feel them breathing down my neck, and it's as if no matter where I go they're already there. I'd say it was ridiculous to think that they were reading my thoughts, but who knows what kinds of tricks they've come up with lately?"

Goose bumps prickled over Fiske, up and around his scalp. "How — how close?" he asked.

Grace shook her head. "I don't want to worry you."

"Grace," said Fiske. "We are hiding out in a hotel in the middle of Washington, DC, after you sent an urgent telegram to my school saying that you were surrounded by Vespers. I think I'm already pretty worried."

"Fiske," said Grace. Her voice was quiet and she didn't look up at him. "I need your help."

"What . . . what can *I* do?" Fiske asked. He wasn't brave, like Grace. He wasn't daring. He wasn't whip smart or cool under pressure. He couldn't even get the kids at school to stop picking on him; there was no way he was capable of saving Grace. Especially if she was this scared.

Grace shook her head, her breath coming in shallow sips. She took Fiske's hand and pushed something cool and hard into it. He looked down at the slim gold ring in his palm.

"Grace? What? No!"

"You have to take it," she said, folding his fingers around it. "They know I'm here, and if they find me, then at least they won't find that. It's the most important thing, Fiske, to keep the ring safe."

"Not more important than you!" said Fiske, shoving the ring back at her. "I don't want it."

"It is," said Grace. "It's more important than me. It's more important than any of us. It's the future of the world there in your hand, Fiske. You have to keep it safe. No one will expect you to have it. And that's how we'll protect it. At least, just for a few days. Until I can shake them. You can do that, can't you?"

"You . . . you want me to take the most important artifact in the world back to school with me?" asked Fiske. His face turned red. "The other day, someone stole all of my socks and threw them into the duck pond, Grace. I honestly don't think it will be safe at school."

"You're not going back to school," said Grace.

"I'm not?"

"I've made other arrangements." She stood up and turned away from him. "I just need a few days. I'll distract them. I'll take them far away from you."

"But if they catch you—"

"Then I won't have the ring. They won't win. Fiske," said Grace, "I need you to trust me, the way that I'm trusting you. I wouldn't ask you to do this if I didn't think that you could—if I didn't think that you had it in you."

Fiske didn't think that was entirely true. He thought she was trusting him because there was no one else she could turn to. Everything in him was pooling in his feet, like he was a bathtub being drained.

"We have to keep it safe," said Grace. "So I'm sending you somewhere safe."

"Where?"

Grace paused. It made Fiske's stomach drop.

"You'll be posing as the grandson of Admiral King. You've met him before—you liked him, remember? You'll have a place aboard the USS *Nautilus*," said Grace.

"What's that?" asked Fiske.

"Oh, well, it's very interesting that you should ask," said Grace. She fiddled with her necklace. "It's a nuclear submarine. The first one, actually. Another Cahill, right on the cusp of history. We're all very proud."

Fiske went pale; he could feel the blood leave his face and a deathly chill rush up to replace it. A submarine? A submarine with a nuclear reactor on board?

"Everything will be fine," said Grace. "Now, what did you pack? Do you have enough clean underwear?"

"A nuclear submarine!" Fiske yelled. "Grace? Really?"

"Keep your voice down!" Grace hissed, rushing to him and clamping a hand over Fiske's mouth. "I'm not kidding, Fiske. This isn't a drill, and it's not some sort of prank. This is my life, and your life, and the future of the world. This is what I need you to do. If you don't . . . then I'm out of options, Fiske. Then they win."

Fiske shuddered involuntarily, and his stomach went cold and turned over. He wished that she could come with him, that she could hide out in a safe place, too.

"Just a few days?" Fiske said.

"Just a few days. You'll be fine. I've taken care of

everything. After you leave here I'll let the Vespers know that I'm on the move again. They won't know that I don't have the ring. I have a fake one to wear in the meantime."

Grace squeezed his hand tighter around the ring. "You'll go to New London, Connecticut. From there, the *Nautilus* is sailing to Puerto Rico. Wherever I am, I'll be monitoring that boat, Fiske. I'll always be watching out for you. And once you're in San Juan, I'll send you word on where to meet me and I'll take the ring back." She paused again. "If you don't hear from me . . ."

"Don't say anything else. Don't you dare finish that sentence."

"If you don't hear from me, then the ring will be yours. To do with what you want. You're the only one I trust with it, Fiske."

Fiske didn't want to cry. He was fourteen years old, for goodness' sake, and far too old to be doing something like that. And he wanted to be strong for Grace. He wanted her to know that she didn't have to worry about him. That the only thing she should do is worry about herself, to keep herself safe.

"Fiske King will be your name on the boat," Grace said. They stood up and Grace grabbed his shoulders and pulled him in for a hug. "You'll be fine. You'll be so fine you won't be able to stand how fine you are. You understand?"

"Please don't die," said Fiske. He couldn't help it. He didn't want to say it; he didn't want to give voice to the idea. "Please don't. If it comes down to anything at all, if you have to make a choice, you make the choice that means you don't die. You understand me, Grace Cahill? You are not leaving me here alone."

"I would never," she said. "Not for anything."

She hugged him hard, then gave him his bag and ushered him out into the hallway, locking the door again behind him. Fiske took a cap out of his bag and pulled it low over his eyes as he made his way down to the lobby and out the doors into a rainy night.

Fiske stood outside of the hotel with his bag over his shoulder and the most valuable thing in the world in his pocket. If he had felt vulnerable before, now he felt as if he was walking around with a giant red and white bull's-eye painted on his back. The street was nearly empty, but he could feel dozens of eyes peering at him, poking at him like razor-sharp sticks.

Grace would flee the hotel via the freight elevator, and he wouldn't see her until next week. Until he resurfaced from his aquatic adventure.

That is, if he resurfaced at all.

The next morning, the morning of May 10, 1955, the world was sparkling. The sun glinted off of the harbor, making the water look like a rolling pool of diamonds. The air was crisp and salty, and even though he was still officially on land, Fiske felt certain that he was about to be seasick.

There she was. The *Nautilus*. As long as one of the football fields at school and made of smooth steel, she was the most incredible and terrible thing that Fiske had ever seen. The hull was dark and matte and half-wet from the lapping water, half-dry from the warm spring sun. Seagulls perched on the antennae and the periscope, all of them admirals in their own minds. Men in bright white uniforms bustled around, hauling coils of rope over their shoulders or heaving bags of potatoes in a long line from a truck to a hatch at the top of the submarine. Boatloads of American-themed bunting hung around and from everything — the submarine itself, the supply trucks, the dock's office doors; Fiske was at least in no danger of forgetting what country he was in. He stood beneath a great patriotic swath above the office door, waiting for a lieutenant and hoping he wouldn't get lost.

All of the activity swirled around in front of Fiske like the whorls in wood around a central knot. The crowd there to see the submarine off was enormous. There were women in new hats and stiff gloves, children with balloons on strings tied to their wrists. Old men yelled at one another to be heard over the sound of other men yelling. The air smelled of salt and fish and people and damp.

Fiske was frozen in place, with no idea of where to

go or who to look at or if he was supposed to talk to anyone. He hoped he wasn't. Because all he wanted to do was get back into the car and drive it straight down to the bottom of the sea.

A pamphlet on the *Nautilus* was twisted in his hands, the paper damp from his sweaty palms. He had been in to the office, had introduced himself as Fiske King, and had had to shake so many hands he thought his own might fall off. Now he was waiting for a man named Herman Oppowitz to show up and help him out.

"Ahoy there!" A short, stocky man in blue coveralls came jogging out of the dock's office. He had buzzed hair, a huge smile, and shoulders so wide he looked like he might be half Texas longhorn. Fiske would have liked him, if he wasn't so scared.

The man grinned and saluted. "You must be Admiral King's grandson. It's an honor to meet you." He stuck his hand out. "Lieutenant Herman Oppowitz. I'll be your chaperone and answer man for your time on the *Nautilus*. Your sea dad, as we call it."

Fiske took his hand; it was so large that it covered Fiske's up to his wrist. "Uh, hello, sir," said Fiske, in a voice so small that it made him blush. "Nice to meet you, too."

"I hear you're awful interested in submarines," said Lieutenant Oppowitz. "That's just great. You know your grandfather served on one back in the twenties? Of course you do. Boy-o, I bet you've got stories. Well, let's get you aboard. Want me to take your bag?"

"No!" Fiske blurted, clutching his bag tighter to his chest. "No. No thank you, I mean."

"Sure thing, kid," said Lieutenant Oppowitz. Fiske could tell he was trying to not look at Fiske as if he was the weirdest kid that the lieutenant had ever met. The lieutenant scratched behind his ear. "So, yeah, let's go on down."

There was a gangplank from the dock to the flat top of the submarine, and then a hatch that was propped open. A ladder dropped down from there, leading into the dark of the submarine. Fiske followed the lieutenant over the gangplank and onto the submarine's top. He expected it to wobble—like he was getting on a sailboat—but it was still and heavy in the water.

"This way, Mr. King!" said Lieutenant Oppowitz, gesturing at the hatch. There was a small ladder to a level platform and then, through another hole in the floor, a much longer ladder that led down into the belly of the boat.

Fiske looked down the hatch at the thirty-foot ladder, swallowed hard, and went down into the deep.

The young sailor sat in the car, a pair of binoculars held to his eyes. "That's him?" he asked. The boy was small and skinny; he'd be easy to find again among the ranks of muscle-bound military personnel.

"Yes," said the driver. "I know it wasn't part of your original mission, but it seems that it's become necessary."

"Don't worry," said the sailor. "I can handle it."

"You have to," said the driver.

"I said I can do it," the other snapped. He flung the car door open and stormed out, grabbing his bag and slinging it over his shoulder. It was heavier than he expected, though, and he nearly dropped it. The driver closed his eyes and shook his head. The sailor flushed a deep scarlet.

"You nervous?" asked the driver. "It's your first mission."

"No," said the sailor. "I'm not nervous at all. I know what's expected of me. I'm fully capable of succeeding."

"Don't forget this," said the driver. He passed the sailor-turned-Vesper a device with a long barrel, a handle, and a trigger. At the end of the barrel were two wires. The sailor took it and stuffed it in his bag. "Remember: Learn everything. And then kill the Cahill."

He nodded. Kill the Cahill. It would be nothing at all, to kill the Cahill.

The hatch was small, and the ladder dropped straight down. Fiske was afraid he would slip and accidentally kick Lieutenant Oppowitz in the face, or fall on top of him. After all, his last try at climbing down something hadn't turned out so well.

"Sorry!" he blurted when his foot slipped, knocking into the lieutenant's hand. This was going to be a disaster. He couldn't even get *into* the submarine without nearly wrecking everything.

"Nothing to worry about," said the lieutenant, pausing to shake the sting out of his hand before continuing down the ladder.

Below, the world was so much smaller than Fiske thought it would be. The ceilings were low and the hallways narrow. Equipment hummed and monitors beeped all around him. He didn't think that Lieutenant Oppowitz would be able to walk down the hall without getting stuck, but the officer moved like, well, a fish in water.

"This is the maneuvering room," said Lieutenant Oppowitz. "Through that door there are the engines. Here is where we control the speed and the propulsion and all of that."

Fiske followed along, trying not to stare. Maybe he wasn't exactly interested in submarines, but that could change. This was a masterful piece of machinery, a perfectly tuned instrument of war. At least, that's what it looked like. It was brightly lit and shining, like a new quarter. Like a very huge, very expensive, very deadly new quarter.

At the same time, it looked and felt almost unfinished. Wires and circuits and screens were stuck out in plain sight, with no panels to cover their guts. Passing people in the halls meant that someone had to flatten himself against a wall.

"This is the nuclear reactor," Lieutenant Oppowitz was saying, and that's when Fiske almost fell over. They had passed through to another room, and there it was: the humming, throbbing heart of the boat. It didn't look like much: just a great metal block with pipes leading in and out of it. He stared at it, and then at his skin, half expecting to see new limbs sprouting up all over the place, or scales, or a clone springing forth. "No need to worry about anything here," said the lieutenant. "There's a lot of steel between you and me and that overgrown battery. We'll make sure you get back to your grandfather in one piece. We're the top two percent of the Navy, Seaman King. No one's going to take a risk at radiating a mind this sharp." He winked and tapped his temple. "Oh, some of the others, sure, but I'm here as a safety measure for all of that. Right? Ha! Right?"

Fiske almost smiled. That was a relief, at least.

"Through here is the mess and the cold storage. You'll be having your meals here, and spending any leisure time. You'll want to be around for meals. Best food under the sea — and above it, too. We don't have too much to brag about down here — it's cramped and dark and let me tell you it'll start to smell after a day or less — but there's nothing that beats the food."

Fiske looked around. The tables were long and

narrow. Everything felt as if it had been shrunk by half. In a way, it was nice. He almost felt swaddled, like it was too small of a space for anything bad to creep into. There was simply no room.

"That through there is the head, and up above there is the control room. Anything that happens down here happens right up there. I'll have to ask you, politely you know, to keep any curious fingers away from any buttons they might want to push. Not that I think you would — but it's a condition of your trip."

"Of course," said Fiske. As if he would want to push any buttons at all. He'd be perfectly content to sit on his bunk for the next few days and not mess about with anything.

Even though he was here — and a full twenty minutes into his mission — he still felt unprepared. Still, there was something about it that was . . . *exciting*. Maybe this was what it was like to be Grace — to be half-terrified and yet half-thrilled. There was something arming about it; something that made him feel like he could do anything.

"This way to your bunk. We're set to launch in about twenty minutes. Exciting, isn't it? I've seen a lot, you know, been around the world a couple of times. But a nuclear submarine! We're going to go the whole way from Connecticut to Puerto Rico underwater. The whole way! I've been underwater before, in the diesel boats, but the whole way — boy, I've never heard anything like it," said Lieutenant Oppowitz. Fiske thought he practically puffed up his chest, like a proud bird about to fly. "And so are you, you know," he added.

"I—I know," said Fiske. Oh, didn't he know.

"This here is your suite," said Lieutenant Oppowitz. They'd traveled down a narrow stairway and were in a skinny room lined with bunks. There was scarcely eighteen inches from mattress to mattress, and only a little curtain to pull for any kind of privacy. Folded on top of Fiske's bunk were two pairs of blue coveralls. "These here are your poopy suits."

"My what?!" Fiske said, trying hard not to giggle. But there was something unmistakably funny about a naval officer saying the word *poopy*.

"Poopy suits," said the lieutenant, his own eyes twinkling with a suppressed laugh. "I know. I can't help it, either. I've got a son that gets a kick out of it, too. Walk-in closet is here," and he lifted the mattress to reveal a small drawer for Fiske's things.

"Thank you," said Fiske, his voice a little squeak. This was happening. It was all really happening. He was going to live on a submarine.

"You don't talk much, do you?" said the lieutenant. Fiske turned pink. "Ah, that's okay. Nothing to be ashamed of. What is it they say? Better to keep your mouth shut and be foolish, or keep it closed and be a fool? Something like that? I don't know. But you're a smart kid, I see that."

"Thanks," said Fiske again, fiddling with the strap on his bag.

"I'll leave you to get your things put away," the lieutenant said. "The other boys have already been down — they'll be getting to their stations soon enough. I'll come and grab you once we're at sea. I've something incredible to show you. We can finish looking around, and I'll be able to answer any questions you might have. It would be a real honor, to be at sea with someone like Admiral King. I'll bet it's just as much an honor to set to sea with his grandson." Lieutenant Oppowitz stuck out his hand, and Fiske took it with a bit of hesitation.

As soon as the lieutenant was gone, Fiske ripped his bag open and set about digging through it. He knew it was in there; he knew because he had laughed when Grace had made him pack it but now it was going to come in so handy he could hardly stand it.

And there it was: a small sewing kit. A missing button didn't seem like it would put humanity at risk, but there was something about the Clue hunt that could make a person look at the world in a different way. Now this sewing kit was going above and beyond its call in life.

Fiske grabbed a poopy suit and the ring from his pocket and as best he could — which wasn't very good, but would do — he sewed the ring into the front of the suit. He stored the other set and his other clothes beneath the mattress; he wasn't going to take the suit off for anything.

He was just buttoning his poopy suit when another

boy entered the bunks. He didn't seem that much older than Fiske.

"That your bunk there?" the boy asked. Fiske nodded, smoothing the creases out of his suit. It was clean and blue and made him feel like a proper seaman. And there was the ring, tugging slightly on the fabric of his suit like a tiny little anchor.

The boy threw his own bag atop a different mattress. "They don't give us much room, do they? Better not have a nightmare or end up sleepwalking, right?"

"Sure," said Fiske, but the other sailor kept talking.

"This your first time going down below?" asked the boy. Fiske nodded.

"It's my first time going down, too. I just graduated from sub school. Of course, there's still a lot of work to do. I'm just a puke. That's what they call the new submariners. It's exciting, isn't it? A nuclear sub, and it's just my first trip. Amazing how they can take something like the bomb and turn it into a way to power things. Not that you could pay me to go near that reactor. I'll be in the control room — far, far away. Very far. Legions. Do you have a specialty?"

"Oh," said Fiske. "N-no. I'm — no."

"Ah, I heard a rumor about you. Well, once you're on a submarine, doesn't that make you a submariner, even just a little bit?" asked the boy. He pulled his mattress back down. "Welcome aboard. I'm sure you'll be a fine addition to the crew."

Fiske blushed and muttered thanks, even though

he was sure it made him look silly and he wanted to look brave and serious in front of the real Navy men. "You, too."

"Oh, well, thank you," said the other boy. "Should we head to the mess? I think everyone is gathering before the launch."

"Sure," said Fiske. "I'm Fiske, by the way. Fiske Ca—King. Fiske King." He put out his hand.

"Nice to meet you, Fiske King," said the boy, shaking his hand. "I'm George."

Fiske and George were making their way to the mess hall when Lieutenant Oppowitz hailed them from the galley.

"Oh, Fiske!" Lieutenant Oppowitz lifted his arm and waved Fiske over. Fiske, feeling rather sailorlike in his crisp blue poopy suit, went willingly. It was easy to slip into a role when you had a costume for it. "We've more of our tour to get on with." He led Fiske off down another narrow hall. "Did you know that the *Nautilus* is the first submarine to have a staircase on it? Look at us! It's like a five-star hotel down here."

Lieutenant Oppowitz charged up the stairs like a rhinoceros and Fiske trailed behind him. It was easy to follow the lieutenant—Fiske could hear him coming and going no matter where his eyes had wandered—and it was easier to like him. He talked enough for both of them, and Fiske didn't feel a need to fill any awkward silences.

The stairs led to the control room. If Fiske had thought that the other halls and rooms in the *Nautilus* had been complex, they were put to shame by the control room. The entire room was bustling, like a giant robot brain that was half-human, half-machine. Every inch of space was telling some sort of story about the boat: the depth, the outside and inside pressure and temperatures, speed and direction, sonar readings, oxygen levels. A sailor not much older than Fiske sat in front of what looked like a steering wheel, his eyes on the small monitor just above the wheel.

Standing in the middle of the crowd was a short man with dark hair and an intelligent face. "Fiske, may I introduce you to Commander Eugene P. Wilkinson, United States Navy," said Lieutenant Oppowitz. Commander Wilkinson stuck out his hand for Fiske to take. Fiske thought he looked like he might be a literature professor, or a man who sold well-made hats, not a naval commander. "Commander Wilkinson is the boss of the submarine, so to speak. If you don't mind my being so informal about it, sir."

"Not at all, Lieutenant. Pleasure to meet you, Fiske King," said the commander when Fiske took his hand. "I hope you understand what kind of privilege you have being down here, young man."

"I do, sir," said Fiske, his voice catching on something dry in his throat. "Yes. Nice to, um, meet you, too."

"A lot of young men would kill for the opportunity," said the commander. "I hope you'll learn a lot while you're down here. I hope you'll be a credit to your family name."

"I—I do, too."

The commander seemed satisfied by this and turned back to the business of the control room. "All right, then. Ranker, the engines are ready?"

"Yes, sir," said a sailor.

"Let's make this a good one. I want to blow them all away. Let's cast off."

Ranker flipped a switch that sent a hum through the boat, and put the radio at his side to his mouth. "Underway on nuclear power."

"We're moving?" asked Fiske. He could barely feel it. He expected the boat to lurch, to plunge down into the depths.

"We sure are," said the lieutenant. He pointed to the sonar screen. A sailor stood with a pad of paper before him and a pencil in hand. He watched the screen and made a note every few beeps. The bottom of the harbor beeped along, alerting the room to every lump of sand, every dip in the seafloor.

Fiske watched in fascination. It was something like a dance, with the commander calling out the steps and each of the sailors stepping around the floor with their screen, their map, their control panel.

It made him feel safe. Nothing bad could happen down here. Someone would notice the moment that anyone was out of step, and then it would be corrected immediately. There was simply no room for error.

Lieutenant Oppowitz called him out of his thoughts, his openmouthed gazing at the control room.

"Ready for something even better?" asked the lieutenant.

"Better than this?" Fiske asked. The lieutenant grinned and nodded.

"There's nothing like it," he said. "Especially the first time you see it. It's my favorite thing, to take a puke up here."

Fiske followed obligingly as they made their way back to where they had first entered the sub. Lieutenant Oppowitz climbed up the ladder, a great dark block above Fiske. And then, with a quick scramble, he was gone. And all he left behind was a pure blue circle of sky.

Fiske followed, and the first thing that hit him was the smell of the air. It was clear, cut through with salt and water. He pulled himself out and he was swallowed up by the blueness of it all.

The *Nautilus* was slicing through the water. The sky above was cloudless and a perfect, clear blue that Fiske thought he might reach up and touch. The wind was strong and he was a bit cold, but it seemed a small price to pay for this exhilaration.

There were no railings around the top of the submarine; there was nothing between him and the rippling water. The nose of the submarine was blunt and round, and it didn't pierce the waves like the prow of a ship. Instead of a crisp slice through the water with a foaming V spreading behind the boat, the water bubbled and rolled away from the hull in great white plumes.

Fiske had to hold his arms out to keep his balance, but the other sailors went about their duties on top of the submarine as if they had grown up on the thing. They checked the antennae sprouting from the periscope tower and bundled up the rope that had held the gangplank in place, but a few of them just stood there to watch the horizon. Fiske couldn't blame them. The wind whipped the loose fabric of his poopy suit around and pitched his well-combed hair into a bird's nest. He felt like a bird, like any moment he would take off and leave the whole world behind. He'd swoop around in the clouds and drop in on Grace, stealing her away from whatever was breathing down her neck.

Grace. His arms dropped. How could he even think of having a good time when she was out there, risking her life for the ring? He put his hand on his chest; it was there.

"They'll want their last bit of good sea air before we're all stuffed down under like a bunch of stinking sardines," said Lieutenant Oppowitz, gesturing at the sailors. "Sometimes I wish we could hover about and do some good fishing. You ever been fishing on the Mississippi, Fiske?"

"Uh, no, sir," said Fiske.

"Best fishing there is. There're people who will try

to tell you that nothing beats the ocean, and sure, it's nice. But there's nothing like that slow old river with your own son at your knee and a worm on the line." The lieutenant threw his arms out wide and waved them back and forth, stretching the muscles in his neck and back. "Won't be able to do that again for some time, right?"

Below, the Klaxon sounded and the sailors began to pull themselves away from their duties.

"That's the call to come on inside," said Lieutenant Oppowitz. "We'll be going down soon. Certainly wouldn't want to be caught out here when that happened!"

"No, no, not at all," Fiske said, hurriedly following the lieutenant back into the boat. Not that he really thought that the sub would go underwater with a dozen of the crew members above decks. But just in case, he wanted to be well away from any doors or hatches when it happened.

The last man down screwed the hatch shut tight. Now, Fiske thought, absolutely nothing else could get into the boat.

It didn't cross his mind that this meant he couldn't get out.

In the mess below, Lieutenant Oppowitz flagged down a sailor and called him over.

"Fiske, this is Petty Officer Third Class Ralph Kane. Everyone has to earn his keep down here, you know, so you'll be helping Ralph out. Ralph is a missile technician. You'll be spending a lot of time in the torpedo room."

Ralph was tall and broad and looked the part of a sailor. He offered a hand to Fiske. "Pleasure to meet you." Though Fiske thought it might not be all that much of a pleasure. Ralph looked a bit annoyed, like someone had just made him the most lethal babysitter under the sea.

"You, too," said Fiske. "But I won't be with you, Lieutenant?"

"You'll be bored stiff with me," said the lieutenant. "Ralph's got the fun job. Not that I envy him, I swear it. My life is exciting enough just being on the boat. I don't need to add torpedoes into it. Ralph here, Ralph on the other hand, he's full of excitement and danger, isn't he?"

"Yes, sir," said Ralph. But Fiske didn't agree. Ralph's face was so serious, Fiske thought his idea of excitement and danger might be rearranging his rock collection.

"Very good," said Lieutenant Oppowitz. "Fiske, you'll be in fine hands. Kane here is a top-notch sailor. Now, I'm off to report for duty. You stick with Ralph and he'll keep you out of trouble."

"Yes, sir," said Fiske, fidgeting a little bit. He didn't feel out of trouble next to Ralph. In fact, he felt very much *in* trouble, except he hadn't done anything yet.

Ralph looked down at Fiske when the lieutenant

walked away. Fiske flushed a deep scarlet and wished that he knew the right thing to say. If Ralph wanted, Fiske was perfectly willing to spend the next four days hiding in his bunk.

"S-so," said Fiske, stumbling around in the awkward silence like a blind man in a fun house. "How deep does it go?"

Ralph looked annoyed again. "Well, if you were a real submariner, you would know that, wouldn't you?" Ralph grabbed a sailor by the elbow—it was George. "Puke, how deep do we go?"

"Uh, uh," said George. He had been just fine chatting with Fiske earlier, but now George's face had turned a strange combination of milky pale with bright red spots. "Uh, that's, uh, seven hundred feet. Sir. Uh, sir."

"Hmph," said Ralph. He turned his deadly serious glare onto Fiske. "This isn't a cruise ship. This isn't a vacation for anyone else. Down here, you're going to have to work like everybody else does. So don't mess around, and don't make me look bad. Got that?"

"Oh, um, sure. Yes." Fiske glanced at George, who raised his eyebrows. Fiske cracked a tiny smile.

And that was a mistake.

Ralph grabbed the collar of Fiske's poopy suit. Fiske's heart jumped into his throat; his only thought in that moment was for the ring. "Look," said Ralph. "I don't care whose grandson you are. Mess around down here, and I'll make you wish you never set foot on this boat. Do you understand me?"

"Yes," said Fiske, his heart beating too fast. "Yes. I understand."

"Good," said Ralph, letting go of Fiske after giving him a shove. "Let's get to work."

Fiske glanced at George again before following Ralph. George gave a little shrug. This was going to be interesting.

Life under the sea was good to Fiske. Namely because people beneath the water were so much nicer to him than his classmates had ever been. Excepting Ralph, sort of. Part of that was probably because they all thought they had to, because he was supposedly the grandson of a World War II hero, but he was willing to look beyond that if it meant some peace.

It was easy to acclimate himself to the structured life on the submarine. There were six hours of sleep on, admittedly, a tiny and not very comfortable bunk. Then six hours of torpedo duty with Ralph. Someone must have told him about "Fiske King's" interest in submarines and to be indulgent of that, because Ralph was full of lectures: about torpedoes and how serious a job he had, about gauges and dials, about the nobility of the submarine.

"Just like a whale," Ralph said. "There is nothing more noble than a whale."

"Sure," agreed Fiske.

"Nothing."

"I agree!"

Since this trip on the *Nautilus* was just a shakedown to get all of her kinks out before taking her out on real missions, there wasn't too much to worry about, in terms of shooting at things. Still, every day, Ralph was there, checking gauges and pressure readings. He arrived for shifts early and was the last one to leave at the end. Fiske thought he probably sang lullabies to the missiles when no one was looking.

After his shift in the torpedo room, Ralph would head to the mess to study. He was nearly through all of his qualifications. One more test and he'd earn his Dolphins—he'd be a full submariner with all of the duty and respect that came with that. Seeing as how he was supposed to be so interested in submarines, Fiske would join him there, as would George when he was off duty.

George was just starting to study for his quals, but he knew so much already. More than Ralph, in fact.

Ralph would stare at a page in his study guide, his mouth moving slowly as he read the words, one by one in his head. George shot off submarine trivia like a rocket, and he sped through his qual calculations and short-answer study questions as if they were the easiest things in the world for him.

The numbers and symbols that George scratched out on paper left Fiske blinking in confusion.

"You could have gone to Harvard," said Fiske. "I

mean, you could have gone to MIT. But you're here."

George shrugged. "I have a duty to serve," he said.

"Wh-what about you?" Fiske asked Ralph. Ralph lifted his eyes, gave Fiske a look, and then went back to his books.

And so far, after two days on the submarine, the ring had stayed a secret. Fiske had been quite serious about not taking off his poopy suit for anything. And though he knew he was beginning to smell, he couldn't be bothered by that. Namely, he told himself, it was because the chemicals on board the submarine that sucked up the carbon dioxide were aversely affected by deodorant, and with a crew of over one hundred men, no deodorant, and very limited hot water supplies, *everyone* smelled.

Fiske was probably the worst of them all. The other guys jumped, yelping, into the icy showers for a few seconds, but Fiske was adamant. He wasn't taking off his suit for anything. But at least he kept washing his hair and brushing his teeth.

He was rubbing a towel over his head when he walked to the bunks. And when he put the towel down, he froze in his place.

His bunk was a mess. It had been thrown open. The sheets had been ripped off and the cubby beneath ransacked. His bag, his socks and underwear, his few toiletries were strewn all over the floor.

Nothing else in the room had been touched.

Fiske's hand flew to his chest, and he pressed the

firmness of the ring into his skin. It was there. It was right there against him—not lost, not stolen.

Still, the sight sent chills up his neck; the skin on his scalp prickled like he had just dunked his head back into the icy shower. Someone had been looking for something in his bunk.

There was no reason for that, unless someone knew who he *really* was.

Fiske wasn't going to panic. He was at least going to try not to. But he could feel his fears jerk awake inside of him, like Frankenstein's monster coming to life. He could taste the shock of adrenaline in his mouth; he could hear a faint buzzing as the hum of the boat faded in and out around him. He wobbled on his feet and had to grab at the nearest bunk to keep from falling over.

He was trapped seven hundred feet underwater with someone who knew his true identity, who knew that he was hiding something, and who was looking for a secret.

Looking for *him*.

Some of the curtains on the other bunks were pulled closed—there had been men sleeping while this was happening. So whoever it was must have been incredibly quiet. George's curtain was pulled, so Fiske jerked it open. If there was anyone who would understand his terror, it would be George.

"George!" he hissed, giving George a fierce shake. George gave a great jerk and his eyes popped open, his arms and legs flying up and down and side to side. He tried to sit up straight and thunked his head hard on the bunk above him.

"What! What?" George yelled. He rubbed his eyes and looked at Fiske with a sleepy scowl. "What is it, Fiske?"

"Look," said Fiske, pointing at his bunk across the narrow gap. "You would have been here. It wasn't like this before. Have you been asleep the whole time? Did you see—did you hear? Anything?"

"What in the . . . ?" George rubbed his eyes and slithered out of his bunk to take a closer look at the damage. "Is that your stuff?"

"Yeah," said Fiske, rubbing a hand over his damp hair. He was spooked and shaking. "I was just in the head and I came back and it was like this. Did you hear anything? You were asleep, I know, but if you did, I just . . ."

"You know," said George. "I might have. I was reading for a bit before I fell asleep and—you know, I heard these footsteps. Heavy footfalls. Like there was a giant in the room. I thought it was Ralph popping in, and I didn't want to hear any of his lectures, so I stayed quiet and kept the curtain shut. You don't—you don't think it was Ralph, do you?"

"Ralph?" said Fiske. Ralph, who always looked so annoyed with Fiske? If there was a . . . a *Vesper* on board, could it be Ralph?

The skin on Fiske's neck prickled as if the Vesper

were there, watching him. Waiting for him. Biding his time until Fiske messed up, looked the wrong way, said the wrong thing — like they both knew he would. And then it would be over. The Vesper would pounce, would take the ring. Fiske would fail.

"Fiske?" said George, tilting his head. "Are you okay?"

"I shouldn't have w-woken you," said Fiske. "Sorry."

"Do you need help putting things back together?" asked George.

"No," said Fiske. "I can — I can do it. Don't, um, tell anyone, okay?"

"Sure," said George. "Your secret is safe with me."

No, thought Fiske. *It's not safe with anyone.*

That night, as Fiske was getting ready to sleep, Ralph walked into the bunk room. He had every right to be there, but that didn't mean that Fiske didn't jump up and clutch his toothbrush to his chest as if it were his favorite teddy bear.

"What?" asked Ralph, and Fiske could have sworn he was baring his teeth when he said it.

"Nothing," said Fiske.

"You know, you don't have to wear that suit all the time, every day. We do have pajamas down here. And showers."

"I'm fine," said Fiske.

"Actually, you smell," said Ralph. "Or shouldn't I talk that way to Admiral King's grandson?" He said it like a challenge, Fiske thought. He didn't believe that story at all.

"You can talk to me however you want," said Fiske. "I don't c-care one way or another." Ralph didn't say anything back to Fiske, but as he was leaving, he made sure to give Fiske a firm shove with his shoulder. Fiske stumbled backward into the bunks, his heart thudding wildly in his chest.

The next morning, though, Ralph was acting as if nothing had happened.

He and Fiske were in the torpedo room, as was expected of them.

"Whales," Ralph was saying, "are fascinating creatures. Did you know that they know what sorts of things they're swimming around just by clicking at them? Beautiful things."

It was near the end of their shift. For six hours, Fiske had been walking on broken glass around Ralph. The only thing that kept him from going entirely crazy was the other sailors on torpedo duty.

"Do you, uh, do you know a lot about them?" asked Fiske. *What benefit would a Vesper have in knowing a lot about whales*, he wondered. Were whales much more vicious than Fiske thought?

"I grew up in Maine," said Ralph. "Right on the coast. Dad keeps a lighthouse, so I spent a lot of time on the water as a kid."

"And then you joined the Navy," said Fiske, carefully edging his mouth around every word.

"Seemed a natural thing to do," said Ralph. "I thought about doing sonar like your friend George there, but I'm not that kind of brain. I guess I'm more on the brawn end of things."

"Come on, Kane," called one of the other sailors. "We're headed to the mess. Jack's made up some of that pot roast and we don't want to miss it."

Fiske stood up and got ready to follow the other sailors. "Our shift isn't over for another three minutes," said Ralph, his gaze sweeping the other sailors and landing on Fiske like an anvil.

"But the pot roast," said the sailor. "Think of the pot roast, Kane. That roast, and the potatoes and carrots and all of that stewing together all day." He rubbed his stomach and made a ridiculous show of smacking his lips together.

Ralph didn't say anything, but he did roll his eyes, which the other sailor seemed to think meant that he was free to take the others and head to the mess.

"Where do you think you're going?" said Ralph as Fiske tried to follow them.

"I—I . . . uh, I, um, pot roast."

"There's three minutes left," said Ralph. "We're staying for those three minutes."

So much could happen in three minutes! Fiske edged away from Ralph. The last of the sailors had skittered off, leaving Fiske by himself with Ralph. The torpedo silo seemed to grow taller, and wider, and deeper, and full of a thousand times more empty space. How far away was the mess? Fiske went over the route in his head. Would anyone hear him scream?

Fiske wanted to run, but he couldn't find the words to make an excuse, and his tongue felt cold and clumsy in his mouth.

On the torpedo control panel, a red light began to blink.

"Shoot," said Ralph, grumbling to himself.

"What?" asked Fiske. Vesper or not, they were still surrounded by missiles. Fiske wasn't sure which one he should be more scared of.

"There's something wrong with number four," said Ralph, looking up. The torpedoes were stacked three high; number four was near the top of the room. There was a narrow ladder that led up to a catwalk just as narrow as the missiles.

"Wrong?" asked Fiske, his voice trembling perhaps just a little more than he wanted it to. "Wrong l-like . . . like how?"

"I don't know," said Ralph. "Easiest way to check would be to go up and take a look at it." He hooked his thumb at the ladder. "Up you go."

"Me!" Fiske cried. "I have to go up?"

"Well, that or you can stay down here and use your vast submarining experience to read these gauges and figure out when the system has stabilized. Sound good?"

"I'll climb up," said Fiske. He pretended like his hands weren't sweaty and slippery against the cold metal of the ladder. He also pretended that three rows of torpedoes weren't that big of a deal.

He tried to fight the vertigo as he climbed, and the sensation that every slight shift of his body weight was going to send him plunging back to the hard metal floor. His heart was jolting around in his chest, as if his panic had knocked it loose from its moorings. Three torpedoes high was actually quite high once you were up there.

At the top of the ladder, he would have to transition to the catwalk. There was a reason that only cats should do things like this, and Fiske suspected it was because they had the extra lives to spare, just in case.

He looked up. Just a bit more to go.

And then the lights went out.

There are no windows on a submarine; there is no chance for so much as a sliver of natural light. When there are no lights on, there is no gradient and no shadows; there is nothing but pitch-black, disorienting darkness.

Fiske froze, his hands glued around the ladder's handles. If he let go, he would fall. He knew it. Something in the darkness would shake him loose, like a leaf in late autumn.

"Fiske! Fiske, are you up there?" Ralph was shouting. "Stay where you are. Don't go banging around. Don't explode anything."

Right. Fiske swallowed. Good plan.

He heard some movement down below. Ralph must have been feeling his way around, searching for a switch, a lamp—something. Unless he was feeling his way toward Fiske in order to murder him in the dark.

Fiske couldn't move. He could only squeeze his eyes shut tight and hope that the lights came on soon.

The Vesper turned on his infrared goggles and locked the door.

The Cahill was clinging to the little metal ladder as if it were his mommy, probably terrified of both the dark and the prospect of being alone with Ralph. The Vesper rolled his eyes. As if the Vespers would try to recruit a mind as thick as Ralph's. If Ralph blathered on any more about his precious whales, the Vesper thought he might vomit right into a torpedo chute.

Ralph was edging toward the door, and the Vesper was easily able to avoid him. Ralph wasn't the target. He wasn't the Boy King they were after. Fiske's eyes were squeezed tight in the dark, and the Vesper watched as he tried to take one hand from the ladder. It took a few tries—as soon as he would loosen his grip, Fiske slapped his hand back against the rungs, reluctant to let go for even just a moment. But eventually, he managed, and made a grabbing motion at his chest. Fiske patted a spot just over his heart, and whatever was there made him visibly relax. Fiske was hiding something, and now the Vesper knew just where.

The Vesper slipped over to the ladder and began to climb.

Fiske was still frozen up there, scarcely able to breathe.

He closed his eyes. Then it felt more like he was blind by choice, rather than by panic-inducing circumstances. He tried to slow his breathing, slow his heavily pounding heart. Did he want to climb down? Ralph was there, and how did he know that Ralph didn't plan it all this way?

"The door's locked," Ralph called up. His voice sounded far away—as far as one could be while in a cramped room on a submarine.

But there was another sound. A closer sound. The sound of the ladder, creaking just the slightest bit. But that didn't make any sense—Ralph was near the door, and Fiske hadn't moved a hair.

Someone else had to be in the room.

Someone else was on the ladder.

Someone was coming for Fiske.

"Ralph?" Fiske called. "Ralph, are you still down there?"

"Stop talking, I'm trying to figure this out," Ralph called back. Did he sound closer? Was he the one on the ladder? Fiske couldn't tell, and he couldn't see. He pressed one hand against his poopy suit; the ring was still there.

"I hear someone coming," said Ralph. He began to pound on the door. "In here! It's locked or jammed or something! Someone come let us out!"

"Ralph, where are you?" Fiske yelled. The dark was so thick it left him in limbo. Nothing was where it seemed or as it seemed; nothing was safe and everything was a danger. Panic was creeping like spiders all over him. Ralph had cut the lights and locked them in; of course he had. Ralph had sent him up so high, so that when the lights went off, Fiske would what—panic? Yes, it had worked. He was going to fall, or accidentally hit something on one of the missiles, and then they would all blow up. He needed to get down, he needed to get out of the torpedo room!

He would climb down. He would hide where Ralph couldn't find him, wouldn't expect him.

"Stay where you are, Fiske, I'm looking for the flashlight," said Ralph. He was close by now; Fiske could tell.

And then, someone grabbed Fiske's ankle and pulled.

Fiske went down, a yelp of surprise tumbling out of him as he landed on top of another body. Fiske flailed and kicked and the person beneath him yelled and flailed and kicked back.

"Are you in there, Kane?" said someone on the other side of the door. "Is Fiske in there with you?"

"Lieutenant Oppowitz!" Fiske yelled. His cheek was throbbing from an elbow hitting under his eye. "I'm in here! Help!"

"Stop kicking! Stop moving!" Ralph yelled back at him. Hands knocked against Fiske, and he could feel someone pulling at his poopy suit. They were feeling for the ring. Whoever was in the dark could see, and they knew where the ring was. Fiske tried to roll away, but someone grabbed his legs and twisted him around.

"Get off of me! Leave it alone!" Fiske yelled. He gave a kick and scrambled away. The lights flickered on a moment later, and Lieutenant Oppowitz stood in the open door, a ring of keys dangling from his hand.

"What is going on in here?" asked the lieutenant. Fiske was scrambling away. He could feel his cheek beginning to swell. Ralph stood up and wiped his bleeding nose.

Fiske. Ralph. And the lieutenant. There was no one else in the room.

"He tried to attack me!" Fiske yelled.

"I did not! You jumped on me!" Ralph said.

"Now, let's calm down," said Lieutenant Oppowitz. "Mr. King, I don't believe that Petty Officer Kane would do a thing like that. I don't believe that for a moment."

"He pulled me off the ladder," said Fiske.

"I didn't," said Ralph. "I didn't touch him until

he fell on me. And then it sure wasn't intentional."

"Are you saying, Petty Officer, that someone else was in the room?" Lieutenant Oppowitz asked.

Both Fiske and Ralph fell quiet. It wasn't out of the question. It was one of the larger rooms on the submarine, with plenty of nooks and crannies in which to hide. Fiske looked around, as if expecting someone to pop up from behind a missile and to give them a little wave. But no one did.

"H-he attacked me," Fiske said again. "He was the only one here. The others had gone to lunch and he made me stay behind so he could attack me."

"That's a lie!" Ralph roared, tensing. Fiske could tell it was taking every ounce of his military training to keep from lunging.

"Fiske," said Lieutenant Oppowitz in a low voice. He took Fiske gently by the shoulder and turned him away from Ralph. "Think about what you're saying. Do you really believe that Petty Officer Kane would keep you around to attack you in the dark? Why would he want to do that? I know he's a little rough around the edges, but I picked him to help you because I trust him. Because he's a good sailor, and that's the most important thing to him. Does that sound like a person who would attack you?"

Fiske glanced between Lieutenant Oppowitz and Ralph, who was so angry he was practically burning with it. Of course the lieutenant couldn't see it; he didn't know what Fiske knew.

"Excuse me," said Fiske.

He left the torpedo room in a hurry, blowing past Ralph and Lieutenant Oppowitz without a glance back. There was no denying it now, no passing anything off as coincidence. Ralph had to be the Vesper.

George was coming out of the head when Fiske grabbed him by the sleeve and pulled him into the cold storage room.

"What? What?!" George cried.

"Quiet!" Fiske hissed at him. "I need your help. I need to trust someone and you've been voluntarily nice to me down here, you know? An-and so I need to ask for your help."

"You do?" said George, his eyebrows lifting. "I mean, you do? What? What can I do?"

"I'm—I'm not who everyone thinks I am," Fiske said. "I can't really—I can't really talk about it. But there's someone here who knows who I am an-and I think—I know—he wants to kill me. I think, m-maybe, you can guess who?"

"What do you need?" asked George. "Do you need me to send a message to someone? Hide something for you? What can I do?"

"I need—" Fiske started. But then Ralph came around the corner.

It was like slow motion, the way he walked down

the submarine's hallway, his iron eyes boring into Fiske and grinding him down into sand. And then, in moments, he was gone again. But Fiske felt like that one encounter had taken years off of his life.

George's eyes flicked back and forth between Fiske and the door that Ralph had gone through, as if any minute he expected armed guards to come bursting in.

"I can't talk now," said Fiske. "But later. We'll talk later. I have to go." He had to get away from everything. He had to go somewhere safe. But he didn't think that space existed on this boat.

"Sure," said George. "I'll keep an eye out."

Fiske nodded and then slipped away. George watched him go and exhaled. And then he smiled.

Fiske took his lunch with the officers that day. Lieutenant Oppowitz, who was too congenial to let the tiff from earlier keep him in a poor mood for long, was more than happy to have Fiske around, as it meant someone else to show off his pictures to.

"That there is Lucy," he was saying, pointing at a very fat baby with very fat blond curls. "She's just barely two now, and quite the little spitfire. And that, that's Peter." Peter was the opposite of Lucy, being stick-skinny with a shock of unruly hair. "He's six. I don't get to see them much, you know. But they send down familygrams whenever they can. My wife, Beth, she writes them, I mean. But the kids send messages. Lucy's started talking. You know what Beth says she said the other day? She said 'Dada.' She did! I'm not even there and she's got me on the brain. What a good little girl, am I right? What a daddy's girl."

"Come on, Herman. The kid doesn't want to hear about your family back in Saint Louis," said one of the officers. He passed the gravy boat. "Tell him about the time you blew something up."

"I don't mind," said Fiske, taking the picture for a closer look. "It must be hard to be away from them for so long." Fiske could sympathize with that. His only family that mattered was never around very often. Fiske thought Grace must be like a shark—if she stopped moving, she would die.

Before, he'd said it as a joke. But now, it was all too great a possibility. Something shook inside of him and he was seized with the need to talk to her. Just for a moment. Just to check and see if she was okay, to hear her voice say that she was fine. He knew that she wanted him to be safe, but it suddenly wasn't fair that being on the submarine meant being completely cut off from her. He handed the picture back to the lieutenant.

"Ah, you know it is," said Lieutenant Oppowitz. He took his picture back and tucked it into the pocket of his poopy suit. "But it's a good job I have. And Beth, I think she likes the quiet. I'm a bit of a chatterbox myself—must be where Lucy gets it, you know."

The chief medical officer, Lieutenant Robinson,

came in then. He looked grim. "Oppowitz, might I steal your boy Mr. King there?"

"What's wrong?" asked Fiske.

"One of the men," said Lieutenant Robinson, "has been attacked. He's asking to see you. Said you might know something about it?"

"Attacked?" said Lieutenant Oppowitz. He looked at Fiske. "And you're involved again?"

"What? I—who? Who is asking for me?"

"Seaman Carmel. George Carmel."

Fiske went pale. Ralph had seen them talking.

"I'll come right away," said Fiske, setting his napkin aside and standing up.

"I'm coming, too," said Lieutenant Oppowitz, his face grim.

They followed Lieutenant Robinson out to the medical berths. Fiske could feel Lieutenant Oppowitz's confusion and anger as he walked. It seeped out of him like water through a sieve.

"Is it bad?" asked Fiske.

"A concussion, I think. Someone hit him on the back of the head. Out of the blue, he says. Petty Officer Kane found him in the hallway outside the control room." Lieutenant Robinson shook his head.

"Does he know who hit him?" asked Lieutenant Oppowitz.

"Says he might," said Robinson. "But wanted to talk to the boy here first."

Lieutenant Robinson opened the door to the infirmary. It smelled of rubbing alcohol and antiseptics, like bleach and the chalk of pills. George was lying on one of the beds.

"Seaman Carmel," said Lieutenant Oppowitz. "What happened? You need only say the word and we'll take care of this right away."

"I don't know for sure, it happened so fast. But I'm pretty sure . . . I think I know who it was." He paused. "Petty Officer Kane." The two lieutenants were visibly stunned by this, but Fiske couldn't imagine why. It was obvious that Ralph would do something like this!

"Kane?" said Lieutenant Robinson. "You're certain?"

"Very nearly," said George. "Fiske can tell you—he's been after me since we set foot on the boat. I don't know why. I think because I'm doing better on my quals. It's not an excuse, of course, but Fiske can tell you."

"Mr. King?" said Lieutenant Robinson. Fiske opened his mouth to agree, but Lieutenant Oppowitz held up a hand.

"Now, wait," said Lieutenant Oppowitz. "I'm the kind of man who relies on the facts in front of him, make no mistake about it. And now I've got two men who say that Petty Officer Kane attacked them within an hour of each other. Now, I know Petty Officer Kane. I've known him since he enrolled in sub school. And the Ralph I know wouldn't do anything like that."

Of course not! Fiske wanted to yell. *The Ralph that you*

know isn't a Vesper! The Ralph you know is working extra hard to look like a sailor so he doesn't get found out!

"I'm going to ask you to think about your story again, Seaman," said the lieutenant, folding his arms. "Petty Officer Kane is the one who found you in the hall. Are you sure you're not just getting confused?"

"No," said George, his face furrowing in frustration. "It was him! I'm not lying. I wouldn't do that. I've got no reason to do that."

The two lieutenants looked at each other.

"I'm telling you, I know Ralph Kane and he wouldn't do that!" said Lieutenant Oppowitz. Lieutenant Robinson sighed. "Don't you sit there and act like you don't know Ralph, either, Jim. He's a good sailor and a better man. Don't you act like he's not."

"I'm just looking at the evidence, Herman," said Lieutenant Robinson.

Fiske wanted to grab Lieutenant Oppowitz by the shoulders and shake him. How could he not see? How could he be so blind to who Ralph really was?

"Your evidence is bunk," said Lieutenant Oppowitz. "Listening to a puke and a kid when you know Ralph just as well as I do. This is a man's life and his job we're talking about!"

"We'll bring Kane to the XO's office and talk to him," said Lieutenant Robinson, trying to inject some rationality back into the conversation. "There's got to be some explanation for this."

"You," said Lieutenant Oppowitz, pointing a finger

216

at Fiske. "You're sticking with me from now on. You're not going to be wandering around on your own. And you're not going to be getting into any more trouble. And whoever is going around attacking my sailors isn't going to get a hand on you, is that clear?"

Fiske could feel himself shrink—he could feel all of his bravery and will coil up on itself deep down in his belly. But he nodded. There was nothing else he could do.

"Well then," said Lieutenant Robinson. He went to the desk and picked up the intercom phone and buzzed the officers' mess. "Robinson here. We have a situation. Yes, Seaman Carmel. Send Third Petty Officer Kane to the XO's office. I'll be right over." And then he hung up. "You coming, Herman?"

Fiske could see the conflict in Lieutenant Oppowitz's face. Yes, he very much wanted to go, Fiske could tell. But he wasn't about to leave Fiske alone. And he certainly wasn't going to take Fiske into the room with Ralph.

"All right, you're sticking with me *after* this. You go back to your bunk and you don't move a muscle until I'm done with this, you understand me? And from then on, you don't leave my side unless you're in the head or asleep, you got that? We've got twelve hours left on this boat and so help me . . . you understand me?"

"I do," said Fiske.

Fiske stayed with Lieutenant Oppowitz for the rest of the day, until it was time for bed. And the only reason they parted then was that there were no free bunks in the officers' quarters.

By the next morning, the news about Ralph and George had spread through the ranks. It was on everyone's mind at breakfast. Fiske had waited for Lieutenant Oppowitz to meet him in the officers' mess, but when he didn't, Fiske went to the crew's tables on his own.

"Well, if it was going to be anyone," said one of the other seamen, a mechanic named Dale, "you knew it was going to be Ralph. You have to wonder how he even got onto the submarine in the first place. If you hadn't noticed, he wasn't the sharpest tool in the shed."

Fiske poked at his eggs.

"I heard he had to go to sub school twice," said another mechanic. "First time he failed out. He had to beg to be allowed to get back in."

"You think you'll go join the Navy, go to sub school after this adventure?" Dale asked Fiske.

Fiske shrugged. He wouldn't really have to, obviously. If he wanted to, he could just ask the secretary of the Navy to let him stay around.

"Going to sub school twice," said the other mechanic with a laugh. "He had to really want it, I guess."

Something pricked in the back of Fiske's brain — something that wasn't right about this whole situation. But he couldn't put his finger directly on what it was.

"Where is he now?" asked Fiske, poking at a pile of

scrambled eggs. The other sailors were quiet, so Fiske glanced up. "I mean, is he—is he in trouble, or . . ."

"Yeah," said Dale. "They made him step off the boat. Play nice or play with the fishes." The other sailors laughed.

"They—they wouldn't really do that?" Fiske asked, glancing around. He knew the answer when the sailors laughed even louder.

"I don't know, he's probably been moved somewhere," said Dale, shoveling a pile of egg and bacon into his mouth. "Might have moved him into the torpedo room. Some of the taller guys would bunk in there if they couldn't fit in their toaster slots of beds."

So he wasn't in custody or a brig or anything like that. Fiske frowned and pushed back his plate—he hadn't eaten anything at all—and excused himself.

The conversation at breakfast had left him feeling exposed for some reason—like he was standing in the middle of a field with no chance of seeing what might come for him out of the trees. He went to find Lieutenant Oppowitz.

He pressed his hand against his chest. Yes, the ring was still there. Funny—it didn't seem like something that would be very important. It wasn't covered in diamonds or precious stones; rings like his were generally only worth their sentimental value. And yet, it was the most important thing in the world.

He would go find Lieutenant Oppowitz, and his last few hours on the submarine would be quick and safe.

That thought snagged him. He ducked into the control room and checked the clocks and the maps. He wasn't an expert at reading them, of course, but even Fiske could tell that they were nearly there.

They were almost to Puerto Rico. He was almost off of the submarine. He'd done it. Well, almost. But he was almost there!

"Quite a trip, isn't it?" said Lieutenant Robinson.

"Oh, um, yes," said Fiske. "Aren't—I mean, should you be in the sick bay?"

"No patients," said Robinson. "My only one checked out this morning. Your friend was fine—nothing too serious at all. It looked worse than it really was. I can't believe we'll be making it to Puerto Rico all underwater. The whole way, Mr. King. We're breaking records."

"Yeah," said Fiske. "Say, have you seen Lieutenant Oppowitz? He wanted me to stick by him and—and I haven't seen him."

"Not since last night," said Robinson. "Have you tried the officers' bunks? He likes to steal a few minutes when he can to write to Beth and the kids."

"Thank you," said Fiske.

From the control room, he went down to the officers' bunks and knocked on the door.

"Lieutenant Oppowitz?" he called. "I heard you were still in here, sir. Sir? It's Fiske King, sir. I have something to tell you."

But there was no answer.

Fiske knocked again, and when Lieutenant Oppowitz

still didn't open the door, Fiske tried the handle himself. It opened easily and he stepped inside.

The room smelled strange. Like smoke; like burnt hair. Fiske stepped inside very carefully. The bunks in the officers' room weren't stacked as high; there was more room to move and to breathe. Lieutenant Oppowitz was lying on the second bunk, high in the last row.

He was dead.

Fiske recoiled. The lieutenant was staring with half-open eyes. His skin looked gray and cold and as if it hadn't been used in a long time. There were two burnt patches on the front of his poopy suit, directly over his heart, where the fabric of the suit and of the lieutenant's undershirt had been burned clear away. His left hand was thrown forward, and the skin around his wedding ring was burned. He'd been electrocuted.

Fiske scrambled toward the door, wanting to scream, wanting to call for help, but unable to do anything except gasp and heave and then throw up in the middle of the hallway.

He was cold with sweat; it ran down his neck and under the collar of his poopy suit. He still felt nauseous. Someone had killed Lieutenant Oppowitz.

Lieutenant Oppowitz was dead.

Lieutenant Oppowitz, who had his wife and Peter and Lucy at home. Lieutenant Oppowitz who had been so nice, and who had just wanted to do an honorable thing and do right by his family, and that's why he was on a submarine. That's why he was taking care of Fiske this whole time.

And he was dead.

Lieutenant Oppowitz wasn't supposed to be the one to die. Fiske was the Cahill; Fiske was the one who was supposed to live with a constant threat of doom. He didn't like it, but he almost expected it now. Lieutenant Oppowitz hadn't been expecting it. He wasn't even on a mission of war right now; he was out with a boat to sail all of the kinks out of it.

"Fiske?"

Fiske had stumbled back toward the control room. There were sailors going about their business, and Commander Wilkinson was there in the center of the room. They were all looking at him. And Fiske opened his mouth. But nothing came out.

"You look terrible," said Commander Wilkinson, coming over to peer at Fiske. "Are you seasick? After all this time? Ranker, go get Lieutenant Robinson."

No! Fiske wanted to yell. *Stop!* He wanted to scream at them all that Lieutenant Oppowitz was dead and that someone had killed him but all of the words got caught behind his teeth and he couldn't make them come out. His face grew hotter and redder and his blood was at a rolling boil as it bubbled through him.

"The l-lieutenant is . . ." began Fiske. He couldn't breathe. He couldn't breathe. He grabbed for his chest, grasping the ring through the fabric of his suit.

"Fiske, spit it out," said George. He'd appeared in the doorway behind Fiske.

"Lieutenant Oppowitz is dead."

The words spilled out of him, hurtling across the control room and smacking each of the men in the face.

"What?" said the commander. "What do you mean—how did he—Robinson! Where is he, Fiske? What do you mean dead?"

"The officers' bunks," said Fiske.

"Someone get Lieutenant Robinson over there right now!" Wilkinson roared. "Someone get the medics!"

"It's too late for that," said Fiske. "He's dead. I saw him. Someone killed him."

Those three words cast a hush over the room. Commander Wilkinson seemed to turn to stone.

"An-and I know who did it," said Fiske. He glanced at George, who turned pale. "Ralph Kane did it."

"Commander, do we—"

"No. Full speed ahead," said the commander, wiping his hand over his wrinkled forehead. "We don't slow down for anything. Washington is expecting us to make a good showing, and we're going to give them that." He turned back to Fiske. "Ralph Kane wouldn't kill Lieutenant Oppowitz. That doesn't make sense at all. Herman was Kane's sea dad. He got him onto the boat. Ralph wouldn't kill the lieutenant. Robinson is going to check on him. He's a doctor, he'll get to the bottom of things."

Everyone keeps saying that, Fiske thought, *but why can't they understand what's so obvious? Lieutenant Oppowitz is dead!*

And he knew who had done it.

Fiske buzzed with anger; he could hear it in his ears and feel it in his skin and it made him shake and it made him burn and freeze at the same time. It wasn't fair. And Fiske was going to do something about it.

Fiske jerked open the door to the torpedo room.

Ralph was there, clipboard in hand, checking his pressure gauges. Fiske took a deep breath, and then yelled at the back of his head.

"I don't know how you did it," Fiske yelled at him. "But I'm here now. And it's just me. So if you're after anything from me you'd better take it now because I'm not letting anyone else die, all right? I'm not going to do that."

Ralph just stared at him. "What are you talking about?" he asked.

"I know what you did! I just found him. You killed Lieutenant Oppowitz! I know what you're here to do!"

"Lieutenant Oppowitz is dead?" Ralph asked. He turned around and dropped the clipboard. "How—I—what?" Ralph came toward Fiske, but Fiske did his best to hold his ground, even though his heart was pounding so hard that it was like drums in his head and his whole skull ached for it. Still, he took a step or two back. "What are you . . . he's dead? How did he die? We're not at war. I mean—was it the Russians? How did . . . what are you talking about?"

Fiske felt his resolve begin to fade. Suddenly, there was that feeling creeping up—like he'd forgotten to put on pants in the morning. Like there was chocolate on his face. Like Ralph had absolutely no idea of what Fiske was talking about.

"You—you're not—?" Fiske stammered. "I mean, you're not a Vesper?"

"A what?" said Ralph. "Lieutenant Oppowitz is dead?"

Of course Ralph wasn't a Vesper. He'd taken his test twice to get onto the submarine. A Cahill would pull strings to get into a place like this. A Vesper . . . a Vesper would be the best of the best. He'd have been recruited. And nothing against Ralph, but big and brawny were a dime a dozen. No, there was only one member of the crew who was light-years ahead of everyone else.

Only one other who could have gone to MIT, or Harvard, but instead had chosen meager pay and cramped quarters.

"A Vesper."

Fiske spun around.

George.

George stood there. He held something in his hand that looked half like a gun and half like a cattle prod. "A Vesper, that's right. Ralph only wishes he could aspire to these ranks, Fiske. Maybe one day, whale boy.

Maybe once you've learned to add past ten while keeping your shoes on."

"Run, Ralph!" Fiske shouted. He took off running as soon as his feet were able to catch up with his brain. Standing around trading barbs with an armed Vesper wasn't a wise thing to do, and Fiske wasn't going to have any of it. He didn't have time to think about where he would go. All he knew was that he couldn't stay here.

Before Fiske had learned that there was a Vesper on board who was willing to kill and before he had to run for his life to escape that Vesper, the *Nautilus* had been an amazing thing. A feat of engineering and art that combined to make something entirely remarkable, practically superhuman.

Now, with his life moments from being over, Fiske didn't see the *Nautilus* as something breathtaking—it was more like an aquatic death trap.

The boat that he had been getting to know was suddenly full of shadows and steam, rattling noises and the grinding of gears. Fiske ran over the metal walkways and climbed ladders and did everything he could to get lost in the maze of metal and piping. Maybe if he couldn't find his way out, then George couldn't find his way to him.

He wished there was time to think back over everything that had happened on the *Nautilus*. He wished that he could tick over every sign that he should have seen coming, every mistake he had made. He wished he could remember if he had given anything away to George about the Clues, about the ring, about Grace. But the only thing he could do was run for his life. There would be time to feel stupid later.

Or there would be time to be dead later.

He could hear George coming — the creaks of the walkways, the sound of heavy breathing — and if he could hear George, then George could hear him. Fiske stopped running. Slowly and quietly, Fiske slipped behind one of the larger steam pipes. He crouched down, keeping in the shadow.

George turned toward where Fiske hid. Fiske could see his shoes on the path. He glanced around. There was nothing to throw at George, nothing to hit him with, if it came to that. There was just Fiske.

"Come on out, Mr. Cahill," said George. He was edging his way down the hall, his head swiveling this way and that as he tried to figure out where Fiske might be hiding. "It's all well and good to put up a fight, but there's wisdom in knowing when to give up. You know what's going to happen now. You're going to come out, you're going to tell me your secrets, and then — well, I'm sure you can guess. Come on."

Fiske crouched all the deeper. There was a small gap — about a foot and a half — between the walkway and the floor. A mess of small pipes and wires ran under it, but Fiske was fairly certain he could squeeze in there if need be. He shifted his weight toward it.

"Come out!" George yelled. "You think I'm going to let you ruin this for me? Do you know what they did for me, Fiske? Your old family friends? You know what they did? They sought me out. That's right. They wanted me. Little Georgie Carmel from Massillon, Ohio. George Carmel who couldn't catch a football or run a mile to save his life but who is a genius.

"And just think of how proud they'll be when they find out how I handled *you*. I was just supposed to tinker with the computer systems, and then, *you* were sent on board the ship. I'd have known you immediately, even if we didn't know you'd be down here." George paused. "You'll make me a legend in their ranks, Fiske. Don't think I don't know you're hiding something, and I'm going to find it. We both know I'm better than you. We both know I'll win."

Fiske bristled, but he stayed put. George was right in front of him now, holding the half gun. Little blue sparks were flashing from the two short wires at the end of the barrel. It looked like a bad way to die.

The lonesomeness of his situation folded around Fiske like a dark quilt. George was going to kill him, and no one would know what had happened. He would vanish in the worst way imaginable — without having said good-bye to anyone. He should have fled to a place where there would be more people — he saw that now, he was so stupid. He should have gone to the control room, where he wouldn't be alone.

But maybe he could still get there. Maybe he didn't have to die in the dark.

Fiske brought his sleeve to his mouth and bit into the thread holding his cuff button in place. His heart was pounding all through his body; it was as if it had turned on an internal PA system and was broadcasting his fear from his brain to his toes. One false move, one noise, and it would be over.

It took a bit of chewing, but soon he'd bitten away the thread. Taking the button from his mouth and holding it between two shaking fingers, he flicked it, like a paper football.

The button flew behind George and over the walkway where he stood, rattling against the pipes. George spun around and stuck his shock gun into the dark. There was a flash of light, and that was the moment that Fiske needed. He slipped down the way, hauled himself up onto the walkway, and began to run.

George spun around and chased after him, the weapon raised. Fiske ran with flashes of light on either side of him as George shot bolt after bolt, shock after shock. The electricity sizzled against the metal, against the pipes and wires all around.

One of the bolts must have knocked into a seam in one of the pipes. It fried the metal, and the pressure from inside was too great. A spurt of water sprang forth, and then another, and then two more. Water sprayed in all directions, soaking Fiske and making the walkways slick and dangerous.

The nuclear reactor hummed ahead. Fiske kept running, even though his lungs were screaming and clawing at him to stop, even though his legs felt as if the muscles in them would tear at any moment.

George fired again. The electric bolt flew just past Fiske's shoulder and crackled over the reactor's control panel. Sparks flew like fireworks, and smoke flared up. The water mixed with the electricity, and the entire reactor began to sizzle and crack. The lights flickered off immediately and an alarm began to wail, softly at first, as if it were just waking up from a long sleep, and then with a ferocity that was almost more frightening than the reactor itself. All of the lights on the reactor's panel turned red and they flickered like the world's most terrifying display of Christmas lights. It was enough to freeze even George for a moment—he seemed unable to move.

The hum of the reactor turned into a groan and a rumble. The boat began to shake. Fiske edged away from it. He wanted to run, but he was afraid to take his eyes off of the reactor, afraid that the moment he looked away, the whole thing would melt.

But he had to go. *Control room, control room*—he repeated it over and over in his head and in his legs. He left the howling reactor and a stricken-looking George and ran.

The control room was grim when he arrived in a burst of breath and panic. Commander Wilkinson frowned at him, and then turned back to barking at his sailors with the radio to his mouth. The siren wailed here as well, and the commander was doing his best to be louder than it.

"All hands — all hands to emergency stations. Repeat: all hands to emergency stations," he yelled, waving his arm at the men in the control room. "Fire up the backup diesel engines; Ranker, you keep this mess of a boat going and don't you stop for anything. We're nearly there. We are nearly there!"

The sailors scattered — most of them headed straight out of the control room and down to the reactor or the diesel engines. Then the commander turned to Fiske.

"Nothing to worry about, Mr. King," he said, putting a hand on Fiske's shoulder and trying to steer him toward the door. "You just sit tight and — and we'll get this sorted out. I'm going to check on the repairs. You head on back to your bunk or the mess and you just sit tight." But Fiske didn't believe him, and he didn't think the commander believed himself.

"Ranker," the commander said, "you're in charge until I get back." And then he left for the reactor.

Fiske watched him go, his mouth hanging open but no words coming out. He couldn't leave! There was so much to tell him — about George and Lieutenant Oppowitz, about Ralph, about Fiske's life hanging in the balance. Whether it was a lack of breath or a lack of courage, Fiske couldn't say. The words stuck to the insides of his mouth and beneath his tongue. More than anything, Fiske wanted to curl in upon himself. He balled his hands into furious fists and curled his bottom lip in between his teeth.

There were only a few men left in the room, but even among them, panic was spreading like a germ.

Fiske felt it, too. Everything had spiraled out of control so quickly that he couldn't even place the moment that things had first started to go wrong. He felt unmoored and adrift in the ocean, with nothing to keep him from washing off the face of the earth.

And now there was no one to ask for help, no one to save him. He'd run to this place for protection, but he felt more alone and more exposed. And if George came—what would happen to the crew? What had happened to Ralph? Fiske's blood was pulsing in rhythm with the siren. The possibility that he might really die, that this crew of men might die because of him, slammed into him and knocked his breath away.

Ralph burst in. "There you are!" he said. "What in the—what is—where's George?"

"I—I—" said Fiske, shrugging his shoulders and trying not to shake like a brittle leaf.

The siren stopped for a moment, and a voice crackled over the intercom in the silence. "Reactor critical. All hands to remain at emergency stations."

"You should be—" Fiske began, but Ralph cut him off. He glanced at the other sailors and then grabbed Fiske's arm, pulling him out into the hallway.

"I saw George, just the same as you did, and I heard

him, too. Lieutenant Oppowitz would have made sure you were safe. And that's what I'm going to do," said Ralph. "Besides, I've known George was no good since he accused me of hitting him. Believe me, any other place but here I would have, but I take this job seriously, and I'm not about to let some puke take it away from me."

Fiske could almost breathe easy because of that. He didn't want to be in the way, but he wouldn't deny that he felt much better with Ralph on his side. Still, guilt slung itself around his neck like a leaden scarf. Lieutenant Oppowitz *would* have done as much as he could to help Fiske.

Now, though, Fiske didn't know what help would look like. The boat might blow up and George was after him, and how was he supposed to make it out of either of those scenarios alive? He felt stupid. None of this would have happened if he hadn't been on the boat to begin with.

"What can w-we do?" asked Fiske, glancing around the deserted hallway.

"Hope," said Ralph.

The submarine gave a great shudder, which had both Fiske and Ralph grabbing for something to hold on to, to keep from falling over. The smell of oil and dirt hit them next, creeping through the air like mist rolling in.

"What's that, what's happening?" Fiske asked, wild eyed.

"They turned on the diesel engines," said Ralph.

"Is that a good thing?" asked Fiske.

"I guess we'll find out," said Ralph. Fiske pressed his hand against the ring. "You keep doing that," said Ralph, nodding toward Fiske's hand.

Fiske scrambled to think of something to say, but he was saved by the crackle of the intercom.

"Reactor stable. Repeat: reactor stable. Relax, boys. We'll make it out of this one yet." The faint sound of cheering echoed down the empty halls, and Fiske felt his body relax for a moment. Jelly rippled through his muscles, and warmth swept over him. But it was only for a moment. Because even if he wasn't going to blow up in a nuclear explosion, he still had a raging Vesper to handle.

A Vesper who would stop at nothing to kill him. A Vesper he couldn't get away from.

"Ralph," said Fiske. "I—I need to get off the boat."

"What?" said Ralph. "You—that's not how submarines work, Fiske."

"No, but I have to," said Fiske. "Everyone is going to stay at their emergency stations for a while, right?"

"Yeah, but—"

"Then George will find me. And he'll try to kill me. And I can't let that happen, Ralph. I *can't* let that happen. Not for me. It's not—it's not for me. Help me get off the boat. Please?"

Ralph looked at him, his face a mud puddle of confusion and concern and sadness. "Why are you down here, really?"

"To hide," said Fiske. "A lot of good I am at that, I guess."

The boys looked at each other for a moment, as Fiske silently begged the sailor to help him escape.

"Come on," said Ralph, grabbing Fiske's arm and leading him through the hallways to the ladder that Fiske had first used to board the submarine. "Climb quickly."

Fiske scrambled up the ladder, driven by adrenaline and fear.

"You might die doing this, too, you know," said Ralph, unscrewing the airtight door to the escape trunk.

"If I die in the water, what I have will die with me. If I die here, and George gets it . . ." Fiske didn't want to shake and shiver in front of Ralph. But he was, and he couldn't help it.

Ralph grabbed a great rubber vest down from a hook. It looked like what the astronauts in B movies wore while exploring Mars or the moon. "Put this on. This is a Momsen lung. Listen to me—are you listening to me?"

Fiske nodded while pulling the vest around his body and buckling it.

"This goes in your mouth," Ralph said, handing him a mouthpiece connected to two rubber tubes that ran around to the vest. "Do not hold your breath. You're going to want to hold your breath. You're out in the middle of the ocean, you're deep underwater, every single part of you is going to be screaming for you to hold your breath. Hold your breath, and you die. You listening to me? Hold your breath and you die. There's so much pressure down here that the air in your lungs is under pressure, too. As you go up, it's going to expand, and if you hold your breath, your lungs will explode."

Fiske went pale.

"You've got to breathe normally," said Ralph, tightening straps and hooking buckles. "In through this tube, and out through the other. Breathe normal. Don't explode. You got it?"

Fiske nodded. Breathe normally. Don't explode.

"See that green button right there?" Ralph said. "There's another one on the outside of the door, too. Hit that green button once the hatch is closed and you're ready to go. If you chicken out and don't push it, then I will. You understand? Get ready," said Ralph. He looked at Fiske. "You might be the bravest kid I ever met. Or the stupidest."

"Probably both," said Fiske. Ralph grinned at him, just for a moment.

"Stupidest," said George. He was standing in the door, sopping wet with submarine water rolling down his temples. His shock gun sparked at his side, half-broken from the water but all the more dangerous for it. "Absolutely the stupidest." He lifted the gun and pointed it.

At Ralph.

"Give me what you're hiding," said George.

"I don't have anything," said Ralph. But George shook his head.

"Not you. Cahill. Give it to me, Cahill. Wouldn't this be just what you hate? Didn't it just wreck you when Lieutenant Oppowitz died? Wouldn't you hate for it to happen again, right in front of you?"

Fiske would. And George knew it, which just meant that Fiske was about as transparent as glass.

"Don't get him involved," said Fiske. "He doesn't have anything."

"Shut up, Fiske," said Ralph, his eyes darting between Fiske, George, and the sparking end of the gun. "It's no use pretending anymore."

"What are you talking about?" said George, turning to Fiske in confusion. "What is he talking about?"

Fiske had no idea.

"We're on the same side," said Ralph. "I'm with you, George. I'm a—a Vesper."

Fiske was stunned into frozen silence. How was that possible? How could he be so impossibly stupid as to trust a Vesper? Again?

"You're what?" said George. "You're on my side? Why? Why are you here? Who sent you? Didn't they think I could do it on my own?"

"That doesn't matter," said Ralph. "I caught him. Isn't that what counts?"

"Shut up," snapped George, his eyes darting back

and forth between the hooded Fiske and Ralph.

Fiske's mind was spinning rapidly out of control as he tried to wrap it around what was happening in front of him. How could he be so stupid? How could he have disappointed Grace this much?

"I caught him first. He's mine," said Ralph, again.

"He's not!" said George. "I've been stalking him this whole time! I killed that officer to get to him! You're not going to take my hard work right out from under my nose." He cocked the gun at Ralph.

"You're really going to shoot your comrade?" said Ralph. "I don't think they'd look very kindly on that. Do you?"

George faltered. "You were going to help him escape."

That was true, thought Fiske. He glanced at Ralph. Ralph was looking at him with steady eyes, an unflinching face.

Fiske wanted to give up. He couldn't begin to put into words how much he wanted to give up. Part of him wanted to just give them the ring—one of them, both of them, it didn't matter.

But the other part knew that there was more to the story. Knew that there was something going on here. That if he could only trust himself, he would figure it out.

"I lied," said Ralph to George. "I was just about to figure out what he was hiding when you showed up. Then I could take it and flush him."

"Well," said George, a self-satisfied smile creeping over his face. "I don't know what it is, but I know where. Take off that vest, Cahill."

Fiske didn't move. He couldn't if he had wanted to, and he definitely didn't want to.

"I know it's in the front of your suit, whatever you have!" George yelled, waving his sparking gun. Fiske shook his head the slightest bit. But George didn't believe that. He marched up to Fiske and grabbed the Momsen lung with one hand, the other pointing the weapon straight at Fiske's face. "I should just fry you and take it for myself."

In that moment of distraction, Ralph darted to the door.

"Breathe!" Ralph yelled, slamming the hatch door shut.

There was a moment of soft quiet.

George had whipped around when Ralph slammed the hatch shut. Fiske's gaze went to the green button, and when George turned back around, his eyes followed there.

"What—"

Fiske looked back at George and then upward at the hatch. He knew what was coming. He knew what Ralph would do.

If Fiske had been scared before, it didn't compare at all to this moment—this moment before the ship opened, and Fiske and George were swept out into the ocean.

Fiske was breathing. His eyes were squeezed shut tight but he breathed in and out, slowly rising to the surface. It was terrifying and surreal. The *Nautilus* sped off and upward, too, rising to the surface as well.

Fiske broke the water with a *pop*, bobbing like a rubber duck. He tore the mouthpiece away and he couldn't help it—he screamed. He screamed in fear and in relief, in sadness and in uncut joy. He'd made it. He'd escaped the submarine. He wasn't dead. He still had the ring. Puerto Rico was in sight. He was above the water.

George was not.

The swim to shore was exhausting, but Fiske was so glad to be off the boat that he didn't care at all. His mind spun with questions, but the physical need to lift one arm and then another, to kick through the ocean, kept his thoughts from wandering too far from the task at hand.

It was a long swim. But so long as there weren't any sharks around, he'd be fine.

Before he was too tired to go on, he felt the sand beneath his soggily sneakered feet and he pulled himself up onto a beach.

His shoes were full of sand and water; his poopy suit not only smelled of salt and fish and seaweed, but it stuck to him like a second skin. Fiske unbuck-led the Momsen lung and cast it aside on the sand. He desperately wished that he had some of that clean underwear that he had left in his cubby on the submarine.

He fell face-first onto the beach, utterly exhausted. There was sand in his mouth, his ears, and every other part of him, but he didn't care. He was never leav-ing land again, not for anything in the world. Fiske rolled over onto his back and spread out his arms and legs, basking in the sun. Alive. He was alive. Mission accomplished.

His hand flew to his chest again, pressing frantically into the fabric of the suit. And there it was.

He'd hidden away on a submarine. He'd kept the ring safe.

His mission was, to all intents and purposes, a success.

But it didn't feel that way. He stared up at the blu-est sky he'd ever seen and he thought about Lieutenant Oppowitz, and Beth and Peter and Lucy in Saint Louis. He thought about the lieutenant's jokes and his sense of duty and pride.

And Fiske realized he was a miserable failure.

Grace had arranged everything, and soon Fiske found himself on a plane headed for Attleboro.

She was waiting for him on the tarmac, and Fiske ran to her as soon as he was on the ground. She wrapped her arms around him in the best big-sisterly way possible; there would be no more danger, no more death for at least the next ten seconds, and that was all Fiske wanted in the world.

"I'm so sorry," she said, taking his face in her hands and giving him a good looking over. "Fiske, I'm so sorry. I can't tell you how sorry I am. I didn't know— I just wasn't thinking straight, and I'm so sorry."

"I'm okay," said Fiske. "I'm really okay. I promise." Still, it was nice to be fussed over. "But how do you know that they won't be waiting for us at home? Or the next place you go?"

Grace cleared her throat. "I took care of it."

"What do you mean you—what happened to your car?" he asked. It had been black before; now it was a blue convertible.

"I had to drive the old one off a cliff," said Grace. "But I like this one better anyway."

"You had to drive it . . . you *had* to drive it off a . . . Grace!"

"I told you I took care of it."

"Grace!"

"I'm fine," she said. "You're fine. Everyone's fine."

Except they weren't. Not everyone.

He and Grace went back home for a few days; after the *Nautilus*, school would seem like a breeze. Still, Fiske needed a few days of simple quiet before he would be able to do anything at all, whether that was a Cahill mission or a geometry exam.

He'd scoured the papers for news of the *Nautilus* crew—of the reactor's breakdown, the death of Lieutenant Oppowitz. But the only thing he could find was an article praising the crew for their unprecedented, record-shattering trip from Connecticut to Puerto Rico.

Still, just because it was in the papers as having happened one way didn't mean that was the whole truth. Guilt still ate at him day and night, and he could feel it sucking at him like quicksand.

And then he had to go back to school, on top of everything.

"You've been quieter than usual," said Grace one morning. It was Sunday, which meant that he'd be flying back to school that night. "I know you've had a . . . a *time* of things, so if you ever want to talk about any of it, you know I'm here for you, Fiske."

He looked at her. He knew she meant it. He knew that she loved him and that she wanted what was best for him. "I just can't believe it happened," he said. "I can't believe that I . . . and that *you* . . . you had to drive your car off of a *cliff*?"

"Yes," said Grace. "But I'm fine. And you're fine.

Everyone is fine, Fiske. You have to focus on that."

"No, they're not," said Fiske, running a hand over his hair. "Grace, you could have died. I could have died. And Lieutenant Oppowitz is dead, Grace. He's not fine. You know he had two little kids? Just little, just barely even—and now he's dead."

Grace looked down at the ground. "I'm very sorry to hear it, Fiske."

"And you know what the worst part of it is? It's not like he died for his country. It's not like he died for something he even believed in, or wanted. He was murdered because we lied to him. You and me, Grace. He thought that I was someone I wasn't, and we told him that. He didn't know anything about the ring, or the Clues, or the Vespers. He's dead because of us. Because of me."

So was George. Fiske tried not to think about it. He hadn't been the one to push the button, to open the gate to the water above, sure. But George hadn't seen it coming. He'd killed the lieutenant and he was going to kill Fiske, given the chance. But did that make it right? Anyone else would think he was crazy for mourning a Vesper. Still, it wasn't something that Fiske could shake.

"No, Fiske," said Grace. She put her hands on his shoulders and squared her face directly in front of his. "They died because of the Vespers. The Vespers, Fiske. It wasn't you."

Fiske looked at her, disbelief carved into his face like hieroglyphs on a tomb. How could she say that? How could she think that it wasn't his fault? Didn't Grace realize that if Fiske had never been on that boat, then the lieutenant would still be alive?

"You kept the ring safe. You kept yourself safe. I'm incredibly sorry about the lieutenant, Fiske, you know I am. But there are things at stake — huge, world-changing risks that need to be taken. Look what you did, Fiske," said Grace. "You were so brave. *So* brave, Fiske. I've never been prouder."

"I don't *want* you to be proud of me for this," said Fiske. "I'm going to send something to Lieutenant Oppowitz's wife. Her name is Beth. We'll . . . I don't know. I can't buy them another dad. I can't go back in time. But I'm going to do something."

"You're a good person, Fiske," said Grace.

But he didn't feel like it.

It was strange, to be back at school. The grounds were still green and the bricks were still red, even though Fiske had faked his way onto a nuclear submarine, traveled underwater from Connecticut to Puerto Rico, avoided being killed by a Vesper spy, escaped from said submarine, and then swam to shore. Fiske didn't think that the sky needed to be orange or anything from now on — things didn't have to be that drastically different — but wasn't something supposed to have changed?

It took him a minute to realize, though, that

something had — him. Before, he had scurried from class to class, from dorm to dining room with his head down and his books clutched to his chest as if all of his guts would fall out if he weren't holding himself together. Now, he looked around him as he walked. His chin wasn't buried in his chest.

It was a small change, but it made all the difference.

He went back to school, but only for exams. On his last day, a package arrived for him. He had to go to the headmaster's office to pick it up.

Sitting at the secretary's desk was a young woman with brown hair and a yellow sweater. "You're Fiske Cahill?" she said.

"Yeah," said Fiske, looking behind him to make sure that there weren't any other Fiske Cahills around. "You're new."

"Oh, yeah," she said, handing over his package. "The other lady had a family thing that she had to leave town for. I hear she was quite the piece of work. Have a nice summer!"

"Thanks for this," said Fiske, holding up the package and walking back outside. He stopped at one of the benches and opened his package. There was a small box and a letter. He opened the box first. It was a shiny silver pin — two dolphins with a rope wrapped around them. The Navy's Dolphins — what Ralph had been working so hard toward.

He opened the letter next. It read:

Dear Fiske,

First off, all is well on the Nautilus. *The nuke boys got the reactor fixed once we reached port and they've assured us that now we'll be able to go even faster. Ranker says it does feel like they juiced it up some, so we'll see. Our official commission is going to happen in September, I hear. I sincerely hope that you'll be able to make it to the New London docks for the ceremony.*

In the box, you'll find your Dolphins. Welcome to the crew, officially. I've got mine now, too. Let's not forget that I had to study a lot harder for mine, but both me and Commander Wilkinson think that you deserve a pair of your own. I told the commander about George being on board to scope all of the nuke stuff and he was going to take it to a shady organization, and that you stopped him. Took him off the boat at a risk to yourself. For being something of a puke when you started, you sure proved yourself along the way. We all say well done to you.

At the end there, I'm sorry if I spooked you. I had to figure out if you were telling the truth, and that's the way that came to me. I don't know or understand exactly what was happening down there, but I'm betting it's way beyond me. Whatever it was, I hope you're managing okay and that everything's going all right.

You're a brave kid, Fiske. If no one ever told you that, now I have.

Keep an eye out for whales,

Ralph Kane, Petty Officer Second Class

P.S. I got a promotion!

Fiske smiled, folded the letter, and pinned his Dolphins to his blazer. It looked awful nice there, all shiny and important.

"Fish! Hey, Fish Breath!" Eric Landry was beneath a tree with his friends. "Where have you been, huh? Get scared and run off after last time?"

"Family business," said Fiske. His stomach still squirmed, and he thought his hands might still shake. He didn't *like* talking to Eric, and he certainly didn't want to get another swirly, but it didn't seem worth it to be afraid of him. It wasn't like he was a Vesper. It wasn't like Fiske was trapped aboard a submarine with him and he wanted to *kill* Fiske and there was no escape.

"Family business, oooh," said Eric. "Sounds serious. Did you go visit your grandma whale, Fish Face?"

"Let me be, Eric," said Fiske.

"No," said Eric. He got up from under the tree and sauntered over to Fiske. "I've missed you, Fish. We have a lot of catching up to do." He dropped his books on the ground and handed his blazer to one of his friends.

"What have you got there on your blazer, Fish? Your gramma's brooch? A fancy lady pin?"

"No," said Fiske. "It's not your business."

"Everything that goes on in this school is my business, Fish Breath. Tell me before I rip it right off of you."

Fiske looked down at his pin, as cool and calm as he could make himself. "It's the insignia for the Naval submarine service."

"What, you steal it from your dad?" asked Eric.

"No," said Fiske. "I earned it."

"Give it to me," said Eric. He reached out and grabbed Fiske's collar. "I said give it to me, Fish Breath."

Fiske looked down at Eric's hand and then back up at him.

"No," said Fiske.

Eric pulled his fist back and scowled his worst at Fiske.

Fiske took a deep breath and cleared his throat. There was nothing to fear in Eric Landry. He wasn't a Vesper. There were way worse things in the world. So he opened his mouth, blinked a few times, and organized the words that he wanted to say.

"You're going to hit me because I won't give you my *pin*?" said Fiske. "Th-that seems like a stupid reason."

Eric's face faltered for just a moment. And a soft ripple went through the crowd of boys behind him. Inside, Fiske was quaking and terrified of being punched in the face. But Eric was just a boy from school.

"It's a pretty stupid reason, Eric," said Fiske.

"Yeah," said one of the other boys. "It's kind of dumb, Eric."

Eric's fist hovered in the air, but he glanced over his shoulder at his friends. Fiske looked, too. They looked impatient, maybe a little annoyed. "Do you want me to pound him or not?" said Eric.

"I kind of want to play football," said Matthew.

"Oh, I call other captain!"

The crowd began to drift away as the teams were divvied up. Soon there was only Eric and Fiske.

"So?" said Eric, dropping his fist and shoving Fiske away. "You're still just a Fish."

Fiske took a step back and smoothed out his blazer. His heart was steadily ticking down to normal, and his nerves were coming off of a boil. He wanted to burst into laughter; he wanted to jump and to yell and to maybe—*maybe*, if no one was looking, punch the air in unadulterated triumph—because he'd stood up to Eric Landry. And Fish? Fish? What kind of insult was Fish?

Fiske glanced down at his Dolphins, gleaming against the wool of his blazer. "Yeah, Eric. I guess I am."